SUBVERSIVES

SUBVERSIVES

STORIES

by Frank Frost

2001 · FITHIAN PRESS
SANTA BARBARA, CALIFORNIA

Copyright © 2001 by Frank Frost
All rights reserved
Printed in the United States of America

Cover design by Victoria Frost-Blanchard

Published by Fithian Press
A division of Daniel and Daniel, Publishers, Inc.
Post Office Box 1525
Santa Barbara, CA 93102
www.danielpublishing.com

LIBRARY OF CONGRESS CATALOGING-IN-PUBLICATION DATA
Frost, Frank J., (date)
    Subersives : stories / Frank Frost.
        p.   cm.
      ISBN 1-56474-374-8 (pbk. : alk. paper)
      I. Title
    PS3556.R5975 S8 2001
    813'.54—dc21
                            00-011834

CONTENTS

The Collectors / 11

Quartzsite / 21

Keep the Change / 35

Mrs. Applewhite / 40

The South Cornfield / 50

The Rabbit Farm / 58

Timmy's in the Well / 81

The Olive Tree / 94

Story Time / 110

Starting All Over Again / 121

The Long Way to Tuscany / 127

New York Jews / 143

The Frampton County Drunk Driver Project / 151

PREFACE

A recent *New Yorker* article on Stephen King speculated why the best-selling author of the last twenty-five years had never been acclaimed for his literary talent. King's friend Dave Barry was quoted saying that Stephen King was in fact a brilliant writer, but he was also a story teller. Everyone in the world loves stories, Barry said, except literature majors, and because literature majors are in charge of what is good and bad in literature, Stephen King is automatically dismissed from any discussion of literary merit.

At the time I read this bit of wisdom I had been trying vainly to sell my stories to literary magazines for three years. Dave Barry's remarks encouraged me to gather up all my favorite stories and publish them in one place with a guaranteed readership instead of knocking at preferment's door among the frigid editors of obscure journals. John Daniel, of Fithian Press, read my collection and immediately accepted it for publication. I am indebted to John, and to editor Eric Larson, for their encouragement and assistance. My wife, Amanda, a skilled writer and editor herself, read the manuscript and assured me that all of Eric's corrections of punctuation and grammar were legitimate.

7

SUBVERSIVES

The Collectors

Professor Mason was standing outside his office, trying to remember. Had he gone down the hall to the bathroom deciding to come back and finish some work? Or had he finished, locked up, and only gone to the bathroom to avoid urgency on the way home? He couldn't remember. There was no light under his door, and it didn't seem important to him, so he walked to the stairway door and began the long spiral down through the stairwell.

Professor Mason always used the stairs, even though his office was on the sixth floor. He reasoned that he got no other exercise. He certainly wasn't going to run around in his underwear, as some of his younger—and even older—colleagues were doing. Nor did he wish to visit a club where he could use strange machines to raise his heartbeat, and smell the sweat of many other people. Besides, he was a historian of science and was aware that until about 1965 no intellectuals had ever exercised. Yet their age at death was quite a bit more advanced than that of other statistical groups, including military personnel, professional athletes, and criminals, all of whom had obviously been required to exercise repeatedly during the course of their lives.

Nevertheless, the professor enjoyed taking the stairs twice a day, or several more times a day if he went to the library or to lunch with a friend or graduate student. The tall, dimly lit tower of the stairwell was featureless concrete, had no association with any other part of his life, and was therefore conducive to concentrated thought as he slowly plodded up and down. He was accustomed to setting himself some specific problem of finite duration, usually the phrasing of a footnote or a slight change in a syllabus, to contemplate on the journey up or down. He was rarely disturbed in his solitary stairwell because the students at his university, although glowing with vigorous Southern California health and wearing expensive running shoes and sportswear, all seemed to prefer the elevator, even to the sociology department on the second floor.

It was rather unusual, therefore, when he heard a door open on the next landing, echoing up and down the concrete tower. He had lost track of the floor he was approaching, having been distracted by trying to remember whether the library computer read umlauts as *fuer* instead of *für* or simply ignored them. Actually, come to think of it, he had been descending for some time.

He rounded the corner of the stairs, and there below him were Morgenstern and Cathcart, one political science and the other anthropology. It wasn't second-floor sociology then. Or not necessarily. They were both looking at him.

"Hello there, Mason," said Morgenstern. "Good to see you, John," said Cathcart. "Shall we walk down together for a bit?"

"Yes, hello, hello. Please join me," answered Mason. "Although it's hard to talk here in the stairwell, it always echoes so."

In fact it was not echoing now at all. *Something atmospheric,* thought Mason.

And then, as his two companions chatted, he remembered something about Morgenstern. Hadn't he died recently? A sudden

The Collectors

stroke on the golf course? Or had that been Morganson, physics? And Cathcart. He hadn't seen him for weeks, even months. He realized he had come to a halt. So had Morgenstern and Cathcart, and they were regarding him gravely.

"I've had a sudden terrible thought," he said.

His companions only looked at him. They seemed unusually sympathetic and concerned for fellow academics.

"I'm dead. That's what, isn't it?" he said.

His companions were silent for a moment. Then Cathcart spoke.

"We've come to walk with you for a while, John. In case you have some questions."

"It's the exercise thing, isn't it? I knew I should have been jogging or something; everyone seemed to be doing it. Although I don't remember anything but standing outside my office. Is it always that way? You don't remember?"

"Not at all, John," said Morgenstern. "You were in perfect health for a man of sixty-two."

"It was quite unexpected. An accident," added Cathcart. "Do you know Drake in your department well?"

"Yes, of course, Renaissance. And the big course in Western Civ. Good Lord! Is he dead too?"

"No," said Morgenstern, "but he should be."

"Yes," went on Cathcart. "He had a crazy student named Cogelshatz who got a "D" from his teaching assistant. Cogelshatz phoned Drake in an absolute rage and demanded a grade change. Drake firmly refused."

"And with his usual bad grace," said Morgenstern. Drake adored children but famously had no patience with lazy college students.

"But what did that have to do with me?"

"It didn't, of course."

"Cogelshatz, you see, got off the elevator on the wrong floor. Drake's office is right below yours. Cogelshatz burst in the right door, but on your floor."

Morgenstern took up the story. "He had picked up a fire axe as he was walking down the hall, and he sank it deep into your skull."

Mason's hands flew to his head.

"No, no! There are no marks!"

"There never are," Cathcart added helpfully.

"But that's terrible!" cried Mason. "And Cogelshatz! What's happened to him?"

"Well. He tried to turn the axe on himself."

"Not at all as easy as with a firearm," added Cathcart with a wry smile.

"No," said Morgenstern. "Poor Cogelshatz made a mess of everything. Western Civ., you, and himself. He'll need extensive cosmetic surgery before his eventual journey to an institution for the criminally insane."

Mason stood silent there in the hall. For they had evidently emerged from the stairway into a long hall, wood paneled, with soft gray carpeting and concealed lighting. He was trying to figure out what he thought of all this. His wife would have been hysterical, but she had died several years ago. His two children lived far away with their own families and called rarely, usually to advise him on investment strategies, advice he never took. He had no research burning to be published, only his long actuarial study of academic lifespans in various scientific disciplines. He had long ago admitted to himself that he didn't care what patterns emerged. But, but, but...

"But what happens now?" he stuttered.

"Ah," his companions said together.

"We're getting to that."

They were walking down the long hall. Now and then there was a door, as if to an office. Once, in an alcove, there was a telephone. As they passed, it rang.

Morgenstern picked it up.

"Hello? Yes, yes...everything is fine—or at least as it ought to be…No, no, he took it very well." He turned to Mason. "I've told them you took it well."

Mason felt a bit cross. "I'm not so sure I've taken it well. You haven't given me much time to think about it. And who in the world are 'them'? And if 'they' are so all-important, why did they let Cogelshatz off at the wrong floor?" He felt himself flush.

"John…I'm sorry. I shouldn't have taken the liberty of assuming anything about your attitude." Morgenstern looked honestly contrite, almost pained, and Mason's anger waned as rapidly as it had risen.

"We'll be off in a bit," said Cathcart, "and the last thing we wanted was to have you upset."

"No, no, I'm quite all right now. It's just that I have no idea what I'm doing, or if I'm going to be doing anything at all."

"Oh, yes, John. In fact you're going to be doing quite a lot."

They had arrived at a glass door looking out at a bus stop. Cathcart was no longer with them.

"Cathcart's off now, John. He's done his bit. And after a little while I'll be taking off too. That's the way it works."

"Could you explain the rules?" asked Mason. "It would help me do whatever it is I'm supposed to be doing."

"John," said Morgenstern, "all we're supposed to do is help our friends over the shock. Then, I assume, everyone's best instincts take over and we act as we always have—ladies and gentlemen helping past friends get used to the idea of…."

"But what happens? I mean, for instance, what happened to Cathcart?" Mason was a little annoyed at himself for sounding nervous and high strung. He wasn't quite sure when his best instincts were going to kick in.

"I have no idea," said Morgenstern. "I just know that during our brief time helping our friends adjust we get this feeling that in some way we are finishing a long, long job and that some marvelous new life is about to start. John, you're about to start your part of the job. Don't you feel it a bit?"

16 Subversives

9

Mason strolled down a path into the park. He was evidently to serve for a little while as a Collector. A sort of interim guide. He had to admit that his colleagues had made the transition less upsetting than it might have been. The trees were in full spring foliage, squirrels scurried across the lawns, and birds hovered above the luxuriant flower beds. Not far away he could see a small lake with swans and ducks going about their business on the surface. A small girl was now approaching from the left along a long avenue of plane trees. When she saw him she started skipping until she was facing him. She studied his face seriously.

"What's your name?" she asked.

"John," said Mason, thinking that "Professor Mason" would be a little formal. "And what is yours?"

"Um...it used to be Debbie. But that's all over. And I'm so happy!" She gave a little hop, then twirled around twice.

Mason had expected someone—probably male—of his age and station, and he had no idea how he was expected to console a little girl, especially one who needed no consoling and who seemed to know exactly where she was. But she didn't need his help to keep the conversation going.

"This is just like I used to dream!" she said. "Back then I had these awful, heavy leg braces. And thick, thick glasses. And my tongue hung out and looked all yucky." She demonstrated, not very successfully. "I was 'suh-vere-ly dee-velop-mentally dis-abled,'" she said, pronouncing carefully. "I could hear, you know, and see a little bit, and feel—mostly hurting. I knew people, like the nurses and my mother when she came to visit. She cried a lot," she confided. Then she tried another twirl.

"But I used to dream, and in my dream I was like this, pretty, and.... Am I pretty, John?"

"You're the prettiest little girl I've ever seen," said Mason. And indeed the little girl had the sweetest face, with long brown hair

The Collectors

17

pulled back in a ponytail. She was wearing a light yellow summer dress in a small flowered pattern, a little too short for her long coltish legs.

"I was always pretty in my dream, and it was sunny and I was in a meadow with flowers, and I could dance and sing. It was marvelous. I always had the same dream. And then this one time I was in my dream and when I woke up I was here. And it's funny, you know, that I know all those words—like 'dee-velop...op...' you know what I mean—and even 'meadow.' I know I never saw a meadow. And now I'm here, and I even know what I'm going to be doing!"

Mason wished he knew what *he* was doing. He wasn't sure he'd be able to speak at all, what with the lump in his throat, as he thought about the awful past life of this little girl, and thinking about his own little girl when she was seven or eight—the girl who was now a thirty-five-year-old mother of three in Portland, Oregon, and whom he'd never see again. But Debbie gave him no chance to speak. She pointed to a hill in the distance.

"Here comes another girl," she said. "She's going to need help. Her mother's boyfriend hit her until she was dead. Isn't that terrible?" she said matter-of-factly, as if a picnic had been interrupted by rain. "And there are supposed to be others. Can you help me when they get here? We can get them all talking, or in a game or something."

Now Mason knew there was something wrong. And as he looked wildly around he suddenly saw a telephone set into a square recess in an oak tree. He'd never seen a telephone in a tree before, except maybe in a comic strip once, but now it seemed entirely natural, and he immediately walked over and picked up the receiver.

"Hello, Professor," he heard a pleasant woman's voice say. "How are we getting along?" He had always been annoyed by the patronizing "we" used by persons who were in no way involved in one's problems, but now he was too concerned to notice.

"I'm afraid there's been a terrible mixup," he said. "I thought we were to 'collect' people we had something in common with, people we could sympathize with and help through their dismay and confusion. But....''

"It's odd you should say that, Professor, what with all your work with children. Could you explain...?''

But Mason suddenly knew what had happened. The poor maniac Cogelshatz was supposed to have killed Drake all along! Drake was to have been the designated Collector. Drake, who adored children. Drake, who volunteered hours every week counseling abused children. Drake, who read aloud to a mesmerized audience of children every Saturday morning in the public library, readings that had been glowingly described in a Sunday *Times* feature story.

"You know, I'm positive it's Professor Drake who's supposed to be here!" he said with some urgency. "All these little girls! When they get here I'll probably just get all upset and choked up and not be able to say a thing! This is absolutely a job for Drake!"

"Well, you know," said the woman. "We *have* been having trouble with this new software.... Let me check back at the last window. Hmm. I'm not really sure how to get there from here.''

"Maybe I can help," said Mason eagerly. Eight years ago he had learned, slowly and painfully, to operate the computer programs so necessary to his statistical studies and now he could even help colleagues with relatively simple problems.

"Oh, I wish you would!" said the woman, with relief. "The person who's supposed to be running this program is away for a while, and I only know how to do it when it's running smoothly.''

"First of all," asked Mason. "Is your computer a Mac?''

"A what?''

"A Macintosh. Uh, does it have a little picture of an apple on it?''

"Oh, I know what you mean. The apple with a bite out of it. No. They didn't think that would be appropriate. But this doesn't have any name on it. Ah! There! I got back to the last window. Now, what was the name? Drake? Uh—oh! It looks like you're right, Professor.

The Collectors   19

His file is highlighted for uploading. But to upload him I'm going to have to delete...."

"No, no, no!" said Mason, hastily. "Don't touch anything for a moment. Let me think...." And he pondered the various programs he knew, the alternative and never very certain scenarios for taking back an action and substituting the right one. Years ago in a fury he had cursed the computer geniuses who had designed programs with no tolerance for wrong steps, and he had wished them all dead. Now, he realized, they *were* dead and were here doing the same thing.

"All right," he announced. "Let's move carefully here. First, drag the current window off a bit so you can see Drake's file."

"Okay, I see what you mean."

"Now activate my file, just click on it anywhere."

He could see Debbie skipping across the grass, going to meet the newcomer. There was a pair of butterflies flirting above her head.

"All right, I've done that."

"Now. What do you get when you pull down your file menu? It should be up at the top there somewhere."

"Let's see. Okay. It says, *new, open, close, save, finalize...*."

Mason was sure he didn't want to be finalized. "Try clicking on *save,*" he said.

"Okay," she said. "This is great, Professor. I'm sure glad you know what you're doing!" Mason was by no means as sure, but he went on doggedly.

"What options do you have under *save*?" he asked.

Up the hill two more girls now appeared, one white, one black. The white girl seemed to be crying.

"It says, *save changes* or *cancel* or *restore.*"

Mason realized he was going to take an awful chance. *Save changes* probably meant that he would be stuck here. *Cancel* just plain worried him. *Restore*, if the programmers had any wits at all, *should* restore him back outside his office, where this all started.

"All right," he said, trying to sound confident. "Listen carefully. Your first step is to bring up *save*. Then click on *restore*. Then when my window disappears, you click on Drake's file and activate him. That should do it. Is that all clear?"

"Oh, it certainly is, and it all makes sense, too, Professor! I can't thank you enough! Okay! Here goes!" Mason saw that Debbie now had two of the new girls by the hands and was leading them his way. They were all smiling and the other girls were tagging along. It was a beautiful day, and he almost wished he could stay for just a bit.

Professor Mason stood outside his office trying to remember. He'd just gone down the hall to the bathroom, but he couldn't remember whether he was coming back to finish something or just to go home. The office seemed to be dark under the door, so he concluded that he had already locked up. Hard to remember when you're trying to recall how the library has catalogued German titles.

He was trudging down the stairwell when he heard a roar and a terrible shriek from the floor just below his. *Students make more noise every year*, he thought. And he went home.

Quartzsite

The powerful Buick flew northward across the Arizona desert, chasing its own shadow with the low winter sun dead behind it, saguaro and ocotillo flashing by.

"Vernon, you're driving too fast, it's making me nervous."

Vern Babcock grumbled a bit, but he slowed down. "Just trying to find a place for lunch. It's almost twelve-thirty."

In Yuma the Denny's had been closed for repairs and they'd been counting on it for lunch. They had a map of the Southwest with all the Denny's marked on it for when they travelled out of the Phoenix area, which wasn't often. Estelle thought that Denny's was the safest place to eat, they were all so clean. They would always get there before noon, for the early-bird price, and have the hot turkey sandwich on the seniors menu, or sometimes Vern would have the roast beef sandwich if he felt daring and he could get Estelle to shut up about his cholesterol.

"Is there another Denny's up ahead?" Estelle asked.

"There might be." Vern Babcock knew there wasn't. His wife couldn't read a roadmap for beans, so he knew she wouldn't check on him. There wasn't as much as a flyspeck on the map until Quartzsite. He'd never been there, but he figured there had to be some kind of hamburger joint he could get Estelle to take a chance on. Maybe even a family restaurant like Denny's. He was getting hungry.

The Babcocks had bought a condo on a golf course outside Phoenix three years ago. Vern Babcock used to own a factory back in Ohio. He'd built it up from just a little workshop after he got out of the army after the big war. Made specialty auto parts, kept up with the technology, and by the time he retired and sold out they had seven or eight annual contracts with General Motors, regular as rain, and he had a good bundle to retire on.

That's why he couldn't figure why they always had to get the early-bird rate, the senior menu, save a few bucks. They had plenty of money, what with the IRA and the factory sale money in a muni-bond fund. But he went along with Estelle and her thrifty ways. Woman'd pull out fifty of those coupons at the supermarket, fifteen cents off the big jar of Miracle Whip and like that, it was embarrassing.

"That must be the next town up there," said Estelle. She had sharp eyes. Vern was looking for buildings and couldn't see any. Just white shadows on the desert ahead. Then they started passing motorhomes here and there, and trailers, just all stuck out there on the desert in no order at all. Vern had to slow down behind a massive Winnebago, and he could begin to see the trailers and motorhomes parked more densely now along the road. It was getting commercial. There were big lots, looked like swap meets, telling you, "Free Parking, Check It Out," signs inviting people to park their RVs, only $4 a day, and then $5, $6 as they went under the I-10 and got into the crowded part of town, and by now they seemed to be right in the middle of Quartzsite, and there were finally real buildings and street signs and a restaurant up ahead, "Harry's," it said, family dining, senior prices. Vern let his wife spot it first, and she did, right on.

Quartzsite

23

"Oh look, Vernon! They got a senior menu!"

Estelle liked the prices on the senior menu, but she crabbed all through lunch about how dirty the place was, she didn't dare order a salad, who knew who'd had their hands on it, so she only had the bean and bacon soup because it'd been cooked enough to kill the germs. *But not enough to kill that gas you'll be passing for a couple days,* thought Vern. He had a club steak sandwich, Estelle so immersed in her own food choices that he was able to get away with ordering a real piece of meat. It turned out overcooked and flavorless but the fries were good and Vern felt full and satisfied after his second cup of coffee.

He asked the waitress, old skinny lady, how come there was nothing but trailers and RVs here.

"They all started coming about ten, fifteen years ago, just a gas station and a couple buildings here then," she said, sounding like a local. "Then somebody started a rock swap meet, other people parked next door and started selling rocks, and soon they all just started parking out there in the desert. No laws against that here in Arizona, not like California." Her tone of voice spoke volumes about the fancy folk of California.

"S'mostly rock shops here now, but you'll find real estate for sale too. Some land here actually belongs to someone." She gave them a smile full of big teeth.

When they started out walking around Quartzsite, looking at the rock shops, Vern knew this was going to drive him nuts. A year ago Estelle had gotten interested in rock hunting because of some of the women in her group at the clubhouse. They'd shown her agates and crystals and stuff like that they'd found out in the desert and how they had them mounted on cards in boxes. To Estelle it became a substitute for organizing all those photos of the grandkids in the albums, with the names and the dates and where the picture was taken, except there weren't going to be many more pictures of the grandkids, them being all grown up and one of them actually in prison…but the rocks found in the desert meant something to her that she could keep doing, something new every day, stuff she could show her friends. And then she heard that at Quartzsite you could find super rocks, and the best prices.

So now she was oohing and aahing at the little baubles they had on all these swap meet kinds of long plank tables you could find, one after another, there in Quartzsite, and she could tell Vern was getting bored, so she finally said, "Vernon, why don't you just wander around by yourself, see if there's anything you want, like a knife, or something?" Vern had bought a fancy bowie knife with a turquoise-inlaid handle a year ago and she was always telling him, "Go look for another knife," as if she figured that was his big deal, knives. It was like with the factory in the old days. Estelle had no idea what they made, and when Vern started to tell her about some major sale they'd made of their new electronic cruise-control module, she'd always change the subject. Now and then she'd say, "Vern, you take such good care of us!"

So they made an arrangement to meet back at the car in an hour and a half, and Vern went walking back the other direction.

Quartzsite really didn't have streets or blocks, except the main street that paralleled the I-10, but there were sort of alleys between all the RVs and the trailers, and now and then a real trailer home. Vern was looking at rocks, rocks, rocks; here was a big hanging of dayglow Elvis on black velvet, now and then a skinned rattler with the fangs wide open, here and there a lady showing paintings she'd made of the desert and the mountains, Vern thinking he'd rather have Elvis on velvet than her painting in his front room. And now he ran into a nice looking little elderly guy in front of a place called Get Your Rocks, who stopped him with a big smile.

"Hey, partner, you look like you're tired of looking at rocks. Wanna take a look in my shop?"

The guy was so friendly, so welcoming, that Vern had to follow him in. Vern had sold stuff all his life, and he tended to trust good salesmen.

Quartzsite   25

They were in a narrow trailer, looking down at a display of rocks, crystals, looked like every other one Vern had seen. He was just about to complain to the proprietor when the little guy put his hands up and said, "Listen, I gotta go for lunch, I'll let Doreen give you the pitch," and Doreen came from the back of the trailer.

Vern thought at first that the woman just had a slip on. Then he could see that it was a very thin, light dress, thin straps over the shoulders, and very short. Doreen had dark, curly hair and full, sensuous lips. Vern had trouble keeping his eyes off the area between her long, bare legs and the clear impression of her nipples under the top of the dress where she didn't seem to be wearing a brassiere. Her whole middle area just seemed to keep moving around. As a prudent man his first reaction was to make his excuses and get out of there. But Doreen moved first. She put a finger under the front of his shirt.

"You've been looking at a lot of rocks?"

"Well, yeah...."

"Let me ask you, did you *get* any rocks yet?"

"Well, no...."

"Okay, big guy, how'd you like to *get your rocks off*?"

Her offer was explicit, and so surprising that Vern looked around rapidly in all directions.

"Hey! Nobody's watching. We'll just go in back there and have a good time. You remember? You remember the last time you really got your rocks off?"

Vern, a businessman, suddenly realized that he was getting a business proposition. It was so surprising that his first reaction was to laugh. But next, obviously, he had to know the price. So he asked.

"Hey, no big deal, big guy!" she responded. "Hundred bucks, which is two, three under Vegas prices. And we take major credit cards."

"Credit cards?" he asked in amazement. "What's your business name?"

"Get Your Rocks Off," she said, giggling. "It's a legitimate business name. We take Visa, Mastercard, no American Express."

The giggle did it.

Vern's life was flashing before his eyes. He figured he hadn't had it on with Estelle for more than twenty years, maybe a lot more. He'd had a quick affair with a waitress back in Tungsten, Ohio, maybe ten years back, but that was it as far as actually doing it with a woman. At the age of seventy he'd thought that part of his life was over. But this curvy woman with the laughing lips sort of put him in a time machine, and before he knew it he was in the back of the trailer taking his clothes off.

It was so much better than he remembered that afterwards he was lying there thinking, *Take me Lord Jesus, now!* But the practical side of his nature, which was mostly what he was, took over, and he thought. *I'll have to try to get up here more often!*

So later on, when he met Estelle back at the Buick and she asked him where he'd been, he said the real estate picture was interesting here, and as a businessman he thought he should look into it. Usually when he mentioned business he could count on Estelle's eyes becoming glazed, but now she looked a little worried.

"You wouldn't invest any of our nest egg, would you, Vernon?" That's what she called the million-six in tax-exempt muni-bonds, their "nest egg."

"Nah, wouldn't touch that. Parcels up here we could make a down payment out of the cash account. Nobody knows what they're doing here. A good businessman could really make a profit. You know, start selling something everybody wants, do some promotion, discount..." and now Estelle's eyes were getting glazed.

Vern made three trips up to Quartzsite to see Doreen, and he thought he'd found just the thing to make his life perfect. He loved Estelle, and he liked just puttering around the retirement community and playing golf now and then, but he'd been getting bored and

Quartzsite 27

his romps with Doreen were just the thing. They put some spice in his life, some spring in his step and even Estelle and some of their friends were saying he looked younger.

So he was crushed the time he came into the trailer and found the guy, Ralph was his name, and Doreen sitting there with long faces.

"Hey, Vern, good to see you. How about a cup of coffee?" Ralph tried to look a little more cheerful. But Doreen didn't seem ready to invite him in back. In fact, she looked like she'd been crying.

"Hey yourself! What's going on here?"

"Well, partner, we're just closin' up shop. Gonna move on some-where—fewer hassles, you know."

"Fewer hassles! Christ, Ralph, I never seen anywhere with fewer hassles than Quartzsite!"

"Yeah. Well. Tell him, Doreen." Ralph just looked defeated, worn out.

"They're raising our rent," she said, looking up at Vern, begging for understanding.

"Raising? They're doubling it!" Ralph broke in. "Bastards told us they can sell the property, so we gotta buy it or pay double rent!"

Vern was thinking quickly. "The owners know the business you're running here?"

"No, no!" Both Ralph and Doreen were shaking their heads. "No. Got nothin' to do with that. Just that we got some prime downtown Quartzsite land here and they got a good deal, they can sell it."

"So how much we talking about, prime Quartzsite land?" Vern was amazed, crummy little place like this out in the desert.

Ralph didn't answer him directly. "Vern, you got three thousand you could get easy, not have to borrow?"

"Why, hell, yeah! Why you asking?"

"Vern, why don't you buy this place?"

Well, Vern Babcock just blew up at that. The idea of buying six thousand square feet, not even a quarter acre—and he was going on and on, how he didn't just fall off the turnip truck, when Ralph added, "And I'll throw in Doreen here."

Vern was going to say he thought they were married and all but Doreen, now looking a little brighter told him, no, it's just a business thing. "You'd probably run it better." And it turned out she owned the existing trailer herself and that was part of the deal.

Later that afternoon Ralph got in his pickup after they'd been to the bank and done all the business. He waved goodbye and he was gone, and Vern realized he'd bought a whorehouse with one employee. He didn't want to think about that just yet, so he and Doreen went in back to celebrate.

Afterward she started in with the ideas and wouldn't shut up, most of them good ideas. Doreen told him she knew a double-wide, real cheap, for sale down the block. They could move it to the lot here and really have a crib, room for four, maybe even five girls. Instead of four, five hundred a day they could be scoring two K, three on a good day.

Vern did the math in his head. Not as good as Doreen was thinking, but it sounded good. They could amortize the land and the double-wide in a couple weeks. Everything after that would be profit.

"But where're we going to get the other girls?" he asked.

"Don't worry your sweet head about that, baby," Doreen said. "I'll go up to Vegas this week, pick up some girls I know. They'd love it here working with old guys like you."

"They'd like old guys?" It didn't make sense to Vern.

"Hell, yeah! I been here with Ralph six weeks, not one old guy didn't have clean underwear and real polite. You think the girls like being there in Vegas, macho creeps smacking them around, pimps beating them up? Some of them are real dopers, like to be around the action, but I know ten girls at least would love to get out of Vegas and start building up some savings, no pimps to pay off, no weirdos. Besides," she said, giving him a naughty smirk, "wouldn't you like a little variety once in a while, all on the house?"

Well, that convinced Vern. He went back to Phoenix, but the next week he was back there in Quartzsite supervising the double-wide being moved onto his new property. And a couple of days later when he went in back with Trixie, one of the new girls, he knew he'd made the deal of his life.

They had an old retired prospector, Dusty, had worked for Ralph before, who would roam the streets and pick up the more prosperous-looking old men, guys stepping out of new Buicks with their lime-green polyester sansabelt slacks. He'd follow them and their wives down the street a bit, and when they split up to follow their own interests, which was inevitable, he'd give the geezer the pitch. Amazing how many of the old dudes would come back to life, follow the prospector back to the double-wide hesitantly, but then, their business done, their rocks properly off, go prancing back down the road, their nostrils flaring. Now and then some uptight old bastard would threaten to call the cops, but they didn't know where the place was, and Dusty would tell them, "Suit yourself pal. But I ain't seen a cop in this town the last ten years. Hee-hee!" And he'd skeedaddle off.

Besides Trixie, a frisky strawberry blonde who needed to fatten up a bit, Vern thought, they had Georgia, a buxom girl with big hair, a black woman named Shawneena, and two sassy little Salvadoran girls, looked like teenagers, who claimed to be twins but weren't. They could get two-fifty or more for their two-on-one act. Deal was, the girls all kept half of what they made, plus tips, which Doreen had told Vern was twice or more what their pimps let them keep in Vegas. And Doreen kept all she made, for running the place and keeping order.

It was a funny thing. The girls were really happy not to be working in Vegas anymore, but all their days off they'd head right back there to see their friends and party and gamble. Vern was happy with them gambling because it meant they'd all be broke after a couple of days and back working. He had a firm rule about drugs, though, so the girls just didn't tell him and kept it cool. Everyone else knew that Georgia and Shawneena were junkies and that Trixie was on speed most of the time she wasn't doing coke. There was some funny cigarette smoke around now and then, but Vern didn't know what it was, he'd never smelled weed in his life, and he accepted the story that they were trying to stop smoking with herbal cigarettes.

Dusty once said there were lots of younger guys wandering around Quartzsite and would they like some of that trade, and all the girls said, "No way, José!" which was Vern's opinion too. He had the normal seventy-year-old's distrust of any male under fifty and was glad to find out the girls had some common sense.

Get Your Rocks Off was a solid success for a month, six weeks, and Vern could tell Estelle he was doing great on those rental properties up there. But it couldn't last. First thing was a big, tubby, happy guy named Harley, a little too young, who visited two, three times, and Caridad, one of the Salvadoran girls was upset.

"Tha' guy, he's the heat, man! I can always tell!" And Shawneena was getting the same vibes. Next thing you know Caridad disappeared.

Her "twin sister" Maria came to see Vern next time he was up there. "Vernon, Caridad she had to spleet, 'cause joo know she's illegal, joo know what I'm saying? Dey catch her, dey gon' send her back to El Salvador. Focking bostards dere, police, dey already kill her modder and fadder!" Maria started crying.

Vern nodded. He figured he was going to lose Maria too.

"So she went to L.A., joo know. An' I gotta go help her dere. We can get work, I know, but I know the English better. Joo know what I mean?"

Vern had always been very fond of Caridad. Now he took out a roll of bills and counted out five hundred—what the hell—a thousand dollars.

"Maria, you go take care of Caridad. And don't let her get arrested, you hear?"

Quartzsite　　31

Maria burst into tears again.

"Vernon, you de nicest mon I ever met, my whole life!" She smiled through the tears. Then she looked at him with pure love in her eyes. "Joo want a queek one, 'fore I go?"

Vern turned it down and drove Maria with her bags to the bus stop before he went back to Phoenix. The whole way home he had this warm, good feeling about himself, and he was humming an old song, Patti Page used to sing it, he thought.

But the next week Doreen looked worried. "I really gotta go to Vegas, get some new staff," she said. "I told Dusty already, don't bring anybody around today."

"Why? What's going on?"

"Well, Georgia and Shawneena finally took off. Y'know, I always figured they needed their...they needed that Vegas atmosphere too much. So now it's only Trixie, and she's up there now, her day off."

"Goddam! We're almost out of business! You better start recruiting fast, hon." Vern wondered if this business was getting too volatile.

"And another thing. That guy Harley was around today, wanting Shawneena. I tell him she's on a break, he goes, 'What are you guys anyway, an L.A. operation?' And I'm like, 'Hey, is that your business or what?' and he starts laughing and saying he's sorry, pretending he's embarrassed or something, but I think he's trouble. What do you think?"

Vern was worried. Doreen had already told him Quartzsite would get too hot in the spring for them to keep going, but he'd been counting on maybe another three months anyway.

"Maybe we should taper off for a bit, see what's going on. Overhead's not that high with the girls gone. Why don't you go on up to Vegas and look around. But don't bring any new staff back until I call you. What's your number up there?"

Doreen told him and drove off, looking relieved. Vern cleaned up the place a little because the girls always left it a goddamn mess and then he was about to leave himself when the door burst open and two men came rushing in.

The first one was Harley, not looking happy anymore, but hard and mean. He put a hand in the middle of Vern's chest and pushed him backward. Well, Vern had always reacted badly to things like that, so he just popped Harley one, knocked him on his ass. Next thing he knew, the next man through hit him on the side of the head with a pistol barrel and Vern wound up sitting on the floor, looking up at this guy in a black suit, holding a big automatic on him.

"Okay, that's enough of that shit. Now let's talk some sense." The man was talking very calmly for an armed thug, Vern thought, painfully trying to get his head back together. Harley was getting up now and he was steamed but the other man just told him to shut up and sit down.

"What kind of sense we talking here?" asked Vern. "You want to rob this place? There's some ladies' clothes, probably dirty. Dishes in the sink. There's a little shit TV and a VCR. The girls are all...."

But the man shushed him. "Forget it, pal, this is business." Vern was going to say something, but then he told himself, just shut up and find out who these guys are, what they want.

"We want to know, is this an L.A. operation?" Vern didn't say anything, looked like he was puzzled.

"You know, are you the L.A. people?" And Vern realized, this guy thinks this is a mob business.

"No," he said, "We're sort of the Phoenix people."

The black suit looked at Harley, who shrugged.

"Well, here's what's going on. We're taking over."

"The hell you're taking over!" Vern was getting hot and thinking about taking away the guy's gun and feeding it to him like he did to a union punk back in Ohio thirty years ago.

"Back off, buddy. We're paying you off. Harley's been around a few times, watched the trade going in, he says it's maybe worth twenty."

Quartzsite 33

Now Vern felt more at home, doing business. He looked outraged. "Twenty! We got at least forty K sunk in this place, not counting next week's payroll!"

Black suit pondered this. He looked at Harley and back, then made up his mind. He took out a roll of bills. "Forget about next week's payroll. We'll take care of that. I'm giving you twenty-five, and that's it. You even open your mouth again and you're in trouble. Tell Phoenix not to come squawking. It's not their jurisdiction. Got that?"

Vern grumbled, but he took the money and put his coat on, getting ready to go.

"And remember this," said Black Suit. "Harley here's a cop, with state CID. Just so you know we're covered, all ways." Harley smirked.

Vern spread out the two hundred and fifty hundred-dollar bills on the breakfast nook table in front of Estelle.

"See, hon? I told you I could make some good real estate deals up there in Quartzsite. About a thousand percent profit!"

"Oh, Vernon! That's...that's...are you sure this is legal? And what about the taxes?" Estelle went on and on, but Vern knew she was already spending it in her mind, maybe not have to go early for the senior menu next time, or buy an agate or something. So then he put down on the table the turquoise-and-silver squashblossom necklace she'd been admiring at the gift shop downtown but wouldn't buy because she thought seven hundred was a fortune and they could never afford it. And he couldn't remember when he'd seen Estelle so happy.

He phoned Doreen, let her know. Then he gave the new owners time to get started in business up there in Quartzsite. He figured a couple of weeks would do it. And then he made an indignant phone call to a Mormon bishop he'd met out on the links, told him about being propositioned in Quartzsite, of all places, and did he know anyone in the law?

A few days later he had to chuckle at the photo in the *Republic* of good old Harley being led off in handcuffs. "State Police Implicated in Prostitution Ring," said the headline. Then a feature story on the same page caught his eye. It seemed that a trailer town had grown up almost overnight on a secondary road outside of Tombstone. Rockshops, antiques, and old gunslinger memorabilia were selling like hotcakes. The photo of the jumble out in the desert looked just like Quartzsite. When Estelle went off to play bridge Vern called Doreen in Las Vegas.

"Hey there, old timer!" she said. "I was wondering if you'd forgotten little Doreen. You probably remembered you were going to split the Quartzsite sale with me, didn't you!"

"That too. But I also think we're back in business again. You game?"

Keep the Change

Mr. Magnus circulated cautiously through the giant Food Bounty supermarket. He hated change. Food Bounty had recently done a demographic survey and found itself surrounded by a large pocket of ethnic neighborhoods. Mr. Magnus and other bewildered white middle-class shoppers now found themselves confronted with strange foods on every aisle. In the meat case they saw new offerings of pork tails and ears, *tripas de leche* in glistening lilac loops, beef tendons. There were strange plants in produce: lemon grass, bok choy, taro root, jars of kimchi and hummus. Worse, the marketing strategy had paid off, and on certain days of the week the market was thronged with small people, generally of a darker hue, always accompanied by swarms of small children sitting crying in shopping carts, otherwise usually out of control, running and screaming up the aisles, bumping into elderly shoppers. The air was rife with foreign tongues, from the familiar Latin staccato, to Middle Eastern gutturals, to singsong Oriental clamor. Even Mrs. Washington, a portly

African-American woman who had been shopping here as long as Mr. Magnus sometimes rolled her eyes at him to express her distaste for the new clientele.

Mr. Magnus had thought that the crowded days coincided with paydays for lower-class workers. No, sneered Edna, the bad-tempered checker, it was welfare check day. Mr. Magnus always tried to avoid Edna, but her line usually seemed the shortest and Holly's was the longest. He liked Holly because when his bill was $8.61, or $12.76 she'd say, "I'll loan you the penny till the next time, sweetheart," and give him a big wink. Mr. Magnus didn't carry pennies, and he made a point of it. Once, when he left three cents behind and explained to the checker that everybody should just round off the price to the nickel, a woman in the line behind him said sarcastically, "They do add up, you know!" He retorted, "If you save ten thousand pennies they'll add up to a hundred dollars. And it takes a hundred dollars a day to live at the poverty level in this town!" Which was true, but he knew he shouldn't have been such a smarty-pants.

Today Edna's line was shortest again, so he went there with his package of skinless chicken breasts, frozen broccoli, and herbal tea bags. The bill came to $6.91 and Mr. Magnus knew better than to try to wheedle Edna out of the penny so he just gritted his teeth and made a point of putting the four pennies back on the counter. An Asian-looking woman behind him said, "You left your change, mister."

"I don't carry pennies anymore," said Mr. Magnus in a smug but good-natured way.

"Hey, I'll take them," said the woman.

"You're welcome to them," he said. But Edna had already raked in the coins and was plunking them in her register.

"Excuse me," said Mr. Magnus, "I told this lady she could have my...."

"Store policy!" snapped Edna. "Manager says we can't leave pennies lying around."

Keep the Change 37

"But he already said I could have them," said the Asian woman, obviously getting angry.

"Too late now," said Edna, slamming the cash drawer closed. "Who's next here?"

"Hey, wait a minute!" exclaimed Mr. Magnus. "I said she could have the pennies, and you just grabbed them up, took them right out of my hand...."

"Come on, for crissakes," yelled a man back in the growing line, juggling two six-packs and three frozen dinners. "Let's get it moving, okay?"

Edna's lips were clamped in a thin slit, and she stared at Mr. Magnus with hatred. Then she turned on the Asian woman. "You wanna check out your stuff, or you think you can get pennies in some other line?"

The woman jerked back as if she'd been slapped. "You think I am begging pennies? How dare you!"

Mr. Magnus was about to chime in, but a big meaty hand came down on his shoulder. It was the assistant manager, a big foreign guy with a black mustache, the guy he'd had trouble with last week.

"What is trouble here? Not coupons again, is it, Edna?"

There had been a misunderstanding last week about an ad in the paper specifying a discount for three soap bars with coupons. Turned out it was only for *jumbo* soap bars, and Mr. Magnus had made a fuss.

"He wanted to give his change to this woman," said Edna, making the word "woman" sound like "third-world slime," "but I already put it in the cash drawer."

Now three more people in line complained loudly.

"She insulted me," shouted the Asian woman. "She called me a beggar! You can keep your goddamn food!" She swept her purchases off onto the floor and stalked out of the store.

"Next customer!" announced the assistant manager loudly, gently kicking her cans and packages under the check-out counter, beckoning to the man with the six-packs. "Step right on up, sir! Is no problems here, folks!" Then he moved Mr. Magnus away from the check-out counter, actually bumping him along with his sturdy belly, and spoke softly but intensely.

"Listen, Magnus, you make more trouble in here and we call police, you understand? Boss will get restraining order in two seconds, keep you out of store. Now you get out, you hear me!"

Mr. Magnus was livid with rage. He couldn't remember being so angry in his entire life. He started to sputter his side of the story, but the manager just kept backing him up until the automatic door hissed open behind him and he had nowhere to go but out.

The Asian woman was named Phan. She got in her old Datsun and drove furiously the seven blocks to her apartment building. It was only eleven in the morning, but her husband, Prin, had been drinking since breakfast. He'd been laid off two weeks ago. He looked up at her with reddened eyes. He was about to warn her not to bitch at him again, but she slammed her purse down on the kitchen table and started talking viciously in their native tongue.

"That filthy sow at the market insulted me, called me a beggar, just over four cents. The same one who made the remark about my food stamps last week. And then the boss threw my food on the floor and told me to get out," she lied.

Prin got unsteadily to his feet. "She what? He did what?"

She told her story again. This time the manager had pushed her out the door and she had almost fallen.

Prin's eyes almost fell out of his head. He stared upward in disbelief, and his hands trembled. Then a horrid curse erupted from his mouth. He dashed into the bedroom, and she could hear him rooting in a drawer. He emerged with an insane grimace on his face and a large revolver in his hand.

"Where are the car keys?" he screamed.

She pointed to her purse. He snatched the keys and slammed his

Keep the Change   39

way out the door. Mrs. Phan silently watched him go, a little smile playing on her lips.

The assistant manager was standing in his cramped station by the window. He heard the Datsun scream into the parking lot and screech to a stop in the middle of a lane of traffic before he whirled and saw a frenzied Asian man scramble out of the car holding a pistol.

"Oh, no!" he said and yelled, "Look out! Is danger! Hit the floor!" Then he reached into the safe and pulled out his own automatic. He had once been in a civil war and was a crack shot.

In the meantime Mr. Magnus had been sitting in his car trying to settle down. He finally decided that he had regained some control and would now be able to speak without stuttering, so he got out intending to give the manager the tongue-lashing of his life. He was almost knocked down by an old Datsun swerving into the lot and lurching to a halt, and he stared in amazement as an Asian man clambered out with a gun and dashed into Food Bounty.

"Oh, boy!" he thought, and followed swiftly, not deterred by the sound of shots.

Prin started shooting the second he cleared the door. He was vaguely aiming at the assistant manager but managed only to hit a black woman and a little Latino boy. The assistant manager took dead aim and drilled him in the heart, killing him instantly. Prin fell, and his revolver went spinning across the polished linoleum floor to wind up at Mr. Magnus's feet just as he entered. Without even thinking Mr. Magnus bent over and picked up the gun.

"It's all right...." he was about to say, but the manager was taking no chances with other crazy people and shot him dead the next second.

Edna was out in back on her break, smoking one of the thirty cigarettes she permitted herself every day since she had decided to cut down on her smoking. She could hear the shots.

"What now?" she wondered.

Mrs. Applewhite

Afternoon business was beginning to pick up at the giant Food Bounty supermarket. From her position, the nearest checkout counter to the main door, Holly always got a kick out of watching the people coming in. Some were reluctant, resigned, ready to buy anything for families who only wanted to stuff something into their faces before returning to the TV. Then there were others who entered with their eyes sparkling, anticipating the treasures that awaited them. Holly saw a woman as broad as she was tall coming in, almost running. An elderly man had his hand on the first shopping cart in the rack, but the fat woman ignored him, twisted the cart out of his hand and almost raced away down the aisles. Holly knew her type. She would show up later at the checkstand with twelve frozen Slim Sweetheart dinners, but she would be eating the last jelly doughnut in a six-pack, girding herself for the ordeal of the Slim Sweethearts—guaranteed less than six hundred calories, whether the sole with broccoli or the turkey breast with summer squash tidbits. She would give Holly a messily written check, smeared with jelly and doughnut grease, that would stick to her fingers and the other checks in the drawer.

Then there were Holly's favorite shoppers, the real chefs, with their veal or duck, Italian parsley, garlic, wine, always ready to tell her what they were going to cook. "Yeah, Holly, I just bone out the duck breasts, coat them with pureed garlic and Dijon mustard, grill them for a few minutes—just like a steak—and serve them with a green peppercorn sauce with cream. You wouldn't believe...!"

And then there was Mrs. Applewhite. This afternoon the regular routine was interrupted for a moment by the shriek of brakes outside in the parking lot. Some of the Food Bounty staff craned their necks to see out the windows. Manny, the hyperactive Chicano bagboy, just jumped up and down, his back to the window.

"Mrs. Applewhite! I betchou a million dollars!"

Arkan Skanderbeg, the assistant manager, was spelling the manager at the raised desk by the window. He could see the enormous old green-finned Cadillac, maybe from the sixties, come cruising down the aisles of the parking lot, never stopping, swerving across lanes, cutting off traffic, until it finally wedged itself at an angle across two parking spaces. Other cars had screeched to a halt in order to avoid the old car, and now drivers were getting out, infuriated, waiting to see who would get out of the Cadillac. At first it seemed that there was no driver at all. Then, when the door opened, they could see that the little old lady was almost too short to appear in the windows of the car. She stepped out, looked around at her audience with a serene smile on her face, then made for the door of the supermarket with a deliberate, bow-legged pace.

Mrs. Applewhite thought that she sort of blended in with the crowd in the Food Bounty. She had a shopping cart that she almost had to reach up to push. She was surrounded by crowds of people who were almost certainly ethnic minorities, she thought, therefore the security people in the store would be watching them, not her. Mrs. Applewhite cruised down the produce aisle and picked up two red potatoes and three onions. Up the cereal aisle, where she collected a box of All-Bran and some corn flakes. She never ate cornflakes but she didn't want people to think she just needed the All-Bran to do...you know what. In the meat case she picked out a slim package of pork chops. Then up in paper products, she got herself a four-pack of paper towels, and paused. This was always the most embarrassing part of her shopping. But she had to do it. She was completely out. So she picked up a package of four rolls of toilet paper, blushing, although she knew no one was watching her.

Actually, they were watching her. Back in the room next to the employees' lounge was a row of closed circuit television sets covering every inch of the store. They had been designed for three security employees to monitor, but for financial reasons the store management had reduced the number to one, and only now and then. No one watched produce. But they always watched the meat case, seeing the shopper looking right and left and then slipping the steaks into a purse or overcoat pocket. It was never a chicken, or stew meat. Steaks. And of course the liquor section was always watched. It used to be cigarettes, but now the cigarettes were all under lock and key since state taxes had made them more expensive, pound for pound, than caviar.

And they watched people they knew were thieves, and Mrs. Applewhite was a thief.

It had been three weeks ago that she wandered into the liquor section. Edna, the bad-tempered checker, had been on duty at the TV monitor back in the employees' lounge at the end of her break. Mrs. Applewhite looked around and took a great interest in little jars of cocktail onions. She made a big production of selecting a bottle and putting it in her cart. At the same time, with miraculous speed, her left hand snapped up a half-pint of brandy on the next shelf and—

Mrs. Applewhite   43

zip—it was in her large purse. Edna yelled in triumph, "We got a live one!" And everyone on break in the lounge ran to see.

"See! That old lady just grabbed a half-pint of some kind of booze and slipped it into her purse!" And she went out to tell Arkan.

Mrs. Applewhite eventually wandered over to Holly's checkout counter. It was the express counter for fewer than twelve items, no checks. Holly was chatting with her last customer.

"Yeah, hon, I know. But what can you do? Now, you have a good evening, you hear!"

She saw Mrs. Applewhite coming up to the counter, putting out her various food purchases and her paper products. Holly knew Mrs. Applewhite's hangups, so she grabbed the toilet paper first and hid it in a plastic bag.

"Hi there, sweetheart! How you doing tonight?"

"Oh, I'm just fine, Holly. Except, you know, the aches and pains. Don't ever get old, dear!"

"I'm doing my best, hon!" By now Holly had swept all the items across the magnetic bar-code reader and had all of Mrs. Applewhite's purchases in plastic bags.

"That'll be eleven-fifty-seven, sweetie."

Mrs. Applewhite was getting a ten and two dollar bills out of her wallet when Arkan walked up to the checkout counter. He was an imposing man, well over six feet and with a big black mustache and an intimidating foreign accent.

"You maybe forgot something in your purse, lady?"

Mrs. Applewhite shrank away. "Oh, my goodness! No, no, no! Why would you say that?"

Arkan simply grabbed her purse, reached in and pulled out the half-pint of brandy. He held it aloft as if it were a strangled child. "So! What is this? You steal liquor?"

Mrs. Applewhite covered her face with her hands and burst out crying. "Oh! No! No! I never meant…!"

A crowd had formed around the checkout counter. The next

person in line, a big burly, red-faced man burst out, "Oh, for crissakes! A half-pint? What could that be? Five bucks or something? Shit! I'll pay for it!" And he waved a handful of money.

Many others echoed him. "Yeah, what's the big deal?"

"It was only a mistake!"

"Come on, man, don't be a Nazi!"

But Arkan was adamant. "No. It is policy. Food Bounty always prosecutes. We saw on monitor in back, how she stole. We called police already."

And here they were, two large men in navy blue, serious as hell, walking into the store, coming up to the counter.

"We charge this woman with shoplifting," said Arkan. "Stealing liquor!" making it sound like a vile and depraved act.

Ten minutes later Holly was on her break back in the employees' lounge, still carrying on.

"I can't believe Arkan, that jerk, calling the cops like that!"

"But you gotta admit, she did steal the bottle!" said Doreen, who'd been watching the TV monitor.

"Yeah, but *cops?* If I'da caught her I'd just tell her, 'Oh, I think you forgot to pay for this, Mrs. Applewhite.' And then...."

"Maybe she's too cheap to pay for her liquor," said one of the bag boys.

"Maybe she's an alcoholic," said Edna. You could always count on Edna for a grim diagnosis.

The door opened and a policeman came in, one of the arresting officers. A burly man with ginger hair and a mustache. Arkan was following him, looking more glum than usual. The cop looked around the room.

"Who was the checker at the counter where Mrs. Applewhite got arrested?"

Holly stood up quickly. "It was me, officer, and it was bullshit! She was going to pay for—"

The officer held up his hand as if holding up traffic for the

Mrs. Applewhite   45

parade of a visiting dignitary. "No. No, no, no. Just one thing I need
to ask. When the manager accused her of stealing the bottle, exactly
what did he do?"

"What did he do?" asked Holly. "I'll tell you what he did, the big
Armenian asshole, he grabbed her purse and took the bottle out of
it. And you know what? She was going to pay me for it, she had just
told me that—"

"Albanian! I always tell you, I am from Albania," shouted Arkan.

The cop held up his hand again, still directing traffic.

"No, no. You don't need to go into all that. You know what it is,
we asked your manager there, the...uh...Mr. Skanderbeg, and he
said the same thing. He took the bottle out of her purse. Thing is,
that'll never stand up in court. Illegal search and seizure. Me and my
partner talked it over with the lady, Mrs....uh...Applewhite, and
we're just going to take her home, going to see she gets home okay.
I don't think she's up to driving that car of hers right now."

"Hey, meng!" cackled Manny the bag boy. "She ain' no tief, but
you chould jerk her focking licence, meng, the way she drive. Almos'
ran my ass over today! Hee-hee."

The policeman smiled wanly. "Well, yeah. Okay, take it easy you
guys." And he left.

Most of the people in the lounge cheered. "Hey, Mrs.
Applewhite!" yelled Manny, and went around high-fiving the employees who responded, like Holly and Doreen. *Whap, whap!* went
the hands, but not Edna. She was still pissed, hoping for a real
prosecution.

That had been three weeks ago, and now the Food Bounty employees who were in the lounge were all clustered around the surveillance
TV, almost as if they were watching a police show.

"See!" said Doreen. "She hates to buy toilet paper! She brought it
up to my stand once in a huge black garbage bag!"

"Toilet paper!" Several employees burst out. Manny was laughing like mad. "Hey, meng! You can do widout every sing in dis store. Every sing—'cept toilet paper. Hey, think it over, meng! Hey! Whatchoo goin' use?" and he went into a paroxysm of chuckles. Edna was in charge of the surveillance, and she almost cackled.

"Guess what, everybody! Applewhite's in the liquor section again."

Doreen, Roy the produce manager, and the others watched the monitor intently. They saw the grainy black-and-white picture looking down from overhead on this tiny woman with a monster shopping cart, standing in the narrow aisle between two rows of shelves and looking around nervously, no idea that the camera tracking her every movement was overhead.

Holly had come into the lounge just in time to see the screen.

"Oh, shit!" she said, and ducked out the door again. No one noticed her go. They were all too entranced watching Mrs. Applewhite's act. She seemed to be gazing at a shelf of cocktail accessories, bottled olives, pickled onions, corkscrews, martini mixing glasses.

"Here goes the old cocktail onion routine again," chortled Edna. And indeed, Mrs. Applewhite went through the entire routine again, carefully picking up a bottle of pickled onions with her right hand, and then her left hand, almost too fast to see, striking like a snake for a half-pint bottle of brandy and slipping it into her purse.

"She slam-dunked that sucker!" said Roy, with admiration. "That old lady got some chops!"

"I'm calling Arkan," said Edna. "This time the bitch is going to the joint!" And as the figure of Mrs. Applewhite exited the screen she turned and picked up the store intercom.

Holly caught Mrs. Applewhite moving down the produce aisle, just by the eggplant.

"Mrs. Applewhite? I gotta talk to you!"

The old lady made an effort to focus through her thick glasses. Then she smiled beatifically.

Mrs. Applewhite   47

"Well! Hello, Holly! How are you, my dear? And why aren't you at your counter?" And she began pushing her cart down the aisle, nervously.

"Mrs. Applewhite, I have to tell you! They saw you take the bottle of brandy!"

Mrs. Applewhite's face froze, and she pushed her cart quickly down the aisle. "I don't know what you're talking about," she said angrily.

Holly grabbed the cart by the push bar and stopped it. She looked around. Luckily they were surrounded by women picking out lettuces, chiles, cucumbers, their children running around, making noises.

"Mrs. Applewhite, I'm only going to say this once! They just saw you on the TV—and she pointed back to the liquor section—and they know you have a bottle of brandy in your purse!"

Incomprehension turned to tragedy on Mrs. Applewhite's face, and she started to cry.

"Oh! Not again? They won't arrest me again? Holly—please—what can I do?"

"It's simple, hon. Just take the bottle out of your purse and put it in your cart and...."

And now it was the old lady's turn to grab Holly's wrist and blurt out her complicated explanation, that in her day a decent woman would never buy spirits, how her maid had once done her shopping and had brought her home just a tiny bottle now and then, and then how all the money situation had changed, she didn't know how, and she couldn't afford her maid anymore, Maria, who had been with her thirty years, and how she needed just a little drink now and then, just for her arthritis, she could afford to buy it of course, but she was so embarrassed—even with the toilet tissue it was so awkward—and a bottle of liquor? She just couldn't do it!

Holly was a smart woman. She got the cart turned around, and they headed back to liquor again.

"Now, listen, hon! Those little bottles are really incriminating! They really look like you're tippling. But you buy a big bottle of brandy, it's the sort of thing anyone would have around—you know, entertaining, even cooking with it, for God's sake!"

They were next to the brandy now, and Holly reached into Mrs. Applewhite's purse and took the little bottle out and put it back on the shelf.

"Now," she said, "I know they're all looking, and I don't care. But let's get you a half-gallon of the store label brandy. Here it is, Food Bounty Napoleon Brand. See, hon, anyone would have brandy on hand, nothing to be ashamed of, and this bottle only costs—let's see—$11.99! See! That's almost eight times as much brandy as the little bottle, and the price is only about twice as much!" And Holly looked up at the TV camera and gave it a triumphant finger.

Arkan was now in the lounge looking at the monitor.

"That Holly!" he said. "She's going to get in trouble!"

"Why you say that?" asked Doreen. "I dunno what she was saying back there, but she stopped the old lady from shoplifting. That's a good move, right?"

"And she made her buy a beeger bottle!" crowed Manny. "She's makin' money for the store, meng!"

As chance would have it, Mrs. Applewhite wound up at Edna's checkout counter. Holly's intervention had put Edna in a worse mood than usual.

Mrs. Applewhite plunked her purchases down on the counter, finishing triumphantly with the large half-gallon of brandy.

"I don't know what I'll do!" she said to the shoppers on all sides. "I've got so much entertaining to do this next week!"

"Hey! I'm coming to your house!" said the man standing behind her, and everyone laughed. Mrs. Applewhite looked around wildly for a moment, then realized that everyone was just joking about her skills as a hostess—having a lot of brandy on hand—so she laughed too. Thank God for Holly, she thought.

Mrs. Applewhite   49

Edna couldn't let it go. "I see you got a lot of toilet paper too!" she said. Mrs. Applewhite blushed furiously.

"Yeah, Edna," said Holly from the next checkout counter. "Four rolls. Would last a tight-ass like you the next ten years!" And everyone around dissolved in laughter again.

Edna would have attacked Holly, but just then the two cops called by Arkan came hulking into the store and marched up to the counter. Arkan came to meet them.

"No. Sorry, officers. We made a mistake. Dere was no shoplifting." And in the confusion Mrs Applewhite quietly paid her bill and left, with Manny bringing up the rear, carrying her bags out to the big Cadillac.

Later on in the employees' lounge Edna started to get on Holly's case again but everyone started yelling.

"Hey, Edna, give it a rest!"

"Yeah, that's a nice old lady!"

"Come on, we all gotta live together! Forget it!"

Two days later they were all shocked by the front page headlines.

"Elderly Widow Found Dead. Overdose of Alcohol Suspected." And the story went on to say that Mrs. Applewhite had been found almost as if asleep in her lounge chair, a smile on her face and a huge empty brandy bottle at her side.

The South Cornfield

I got back on the bus from Atlanta around eleven and saw Jimmy Willis just leaving the post office in his pickup. So he gave me a ride down the road, and I guess it was lunchtime when I got to the house, went out in the kitchen right away to tell Ma. She saw me coming, she wasn't smiling or nothing, just standing there holding a dish she was wiping, and she put up a hand.

"Now, don't tell me anything, don't say anything. You got to go tell your father first, he's down in the south cornfield, plowing."

I hugged her anyway, the poor tired woman, looking so beat, like she was caught in a trap that took all the fight out of her. I saw a fox like that, Pa had put out the traps 'cause we'd lost some chickens but he'd never check 'em ever' day like you should, and I found the animal down by the bluff, had been in the trap maybe a couple of days and looked up at me so calm like he was saying, "please shoot me."

The tractor was raising dust by the river, and Pa was making furrows outward toward Indian bluff over the big bend where the river

The South Cornfield   51

comes west again. I had to walk over the whole cornfield, and he wouldn't stop the tractor until he practically had to run over me. Then he just let her idle and looked down at me, grim as usual, that big stringy man, raggedy hat on his head against the sun. I was a big boy and my bud, five years older, was even bigger, but Pa was so strong you'd feel that grip on you and you'd go all weak and just take your whipping. I started talking up a storm, trying to make it as happy and exciting as I'd felt that morning.

"I got accepted, Pa! Full scholarship for four years! And they said I'll have a part-time job the whole time, be able to send some money home even!"

He wiped his forehead with that big red bandana and then pinched his nose and blew it, get the dust out of there. He didn't say nothing for a minute.

Then, "So you're going to play football with niggers, is that it?"

"Oh, Pa! It's an engineering major! I'm going to get an engineering degree, you know, we talked about it? How Ma always wanted me to go to college? And State gave me the interview? But I didn't have the grades…it was always the football scholarship, was going to pay for it!"

"Playing games with niggers, that's all it ever was. You can figure out some way of paying the college. You set one foot on that football field and you're not welcome here anymore. I won't want you to talk to your mother anymore, your bud, your sister. You can just leave and play with your nigger friends. Now get out of here. Some of us got work to do."

And he looked so crazy I just left, went back to the house and sat down at the big table in the kitchen. I was hoping against hope that Ma would ask me what was wrong so I could let it out, all the pressure I had inside, about being able to go to college, what I'd dreamed about the last four years, and playing football there at State.

My bud came and sat down. His name's Traxton—Dad named him after a state senator who stood somewhere with a shotgun to keep black kids from going in a schoolroom back in those bad old days. Black kids, I guess they say African-Americans now. I don't say the "N" word. Ma doesn't either, or any of us but Pa. I keep thinking, that stuff's all over, let's get on with it, you know? My name's Wallace, I guess you can figure that out, where that came from, but everybody calls me Wally, even Pa, since he decided the governor had sold out.

In a bit my sister Maryann came and sat down. She's only fifteen. We're all sort of a quiet family when Pa's around, but she's the only one who'll speak up, argue with him without him getting mad, and we're all sitting around like little mice pretending we're not even there and she's going, "But Pa! That doesn't make sense!" or something else that if Trax or I said it we'd get a big hand up alongside our head.

Anyway, Pa wasn't there and Ma said he was going to finish the field and we should eat, which was pork chops and greens. We eat a lot of pork 'cause that's what we raise, it's mostly a hog farm, and that's why Pa gets so intense about the cornfield. Since he's started he's been trying to grow enough corn so we don't have to buy feed for the hogs, maybe even have some left over to sell in the neighborhood. He's hell on wheels about not having to buy anything to keep the farm going. I guess it's old habits.

Maryann was like jumping up and down.

"Did you get the scholarship, Wally?"

"Yeah, I did, Sis, the whole four years."

"Well, what's wrong? You don't look very happy!"

And I was going to tell her, but I got emotional and I started crying instead and then they all heard what Pa'd said about playing on a team with black guys.

"That's the dumbest thing I ever heard!" said Maryann. And Ma spoke up, real stern, "Don't you ever call your father dumb, you hear!" and we all knew if me or Traxton had said it Ma would have caught us one on the ear, but she was always gentle with Maryann. Then Ma looked at me.

The South Cornfield

"Wally, your pa can be hard sometimes, and you know we all want you to go to State. I'll talk to him this afternoon, time he gets finished with the cornfield, and we'll see what happens."

Well, that afternoon we all had our chores, and after Maryann and I got through with the hogs—feeding, and watering their mudhole, cause it had been dry last few weeks and it was getting hot, they needed their mud and their shade—she told me about the Indian stuff down by the river. So we went down there, by Indian bluff, and she showed me where the big rains last month had brought the river up under the bluff and undercut it and there was a cave there now where there'd only been a cliff long as I could remember.

"See, Wally, up here in the wall? There's bones and stuff sticking out! Do you think it's real old?"

"Me? I don't know. You gotta get one of the archaeologists out here from the university, do some tests. Maybe they could date the bones. They don't look like human to me, probably animals the Indians ate. But they could tell."

"Sure! Can you see Pa letting archaeologists on our property? He'd be afraid the government would shut us down, take our farm away!"

Well, there wasn't any arguing with that. That was our father, in a nutshell. But I was worried about something else. "You know, Sis, I don't think Pa knows the bluff got undercut like this. He's been plowing a lot closer to the big oak tree up there than he usually does."

"Well, we'll tell him tonight at dinner."

Pa worked until the sun went down, and then he didn't even wash when he came in to dinner. That was strange, 'cause he always worked harder and longer than anyone I know, but he would always wash, come in to dinner looking pale, wearing a fresh shirt and pants, and usually grinning a little, as if he was saying to us, "You own a farm you gotta work it." And we'd talk and joke about the work we'd all done that day. But tonight he was grim, and his hands and face were dirty, and he started right in on us.

"I guess everybody thinks it's easy here, running this farm." And we're all saying, real serious, "No, no, not us Pa, we know it's hard…"

"Wally here wants to go to the State College, and play games. I can understand that. I'd like to play some games sometime in my life." And we all shut up.

"You did real good in high school, didn't you, son?"

"Yes sir. Still doing good. They say I'll have a three-point-five next month when I graduate."

"A three-point-five. I don't know what that is but I guess it's good. And playing baseball, too."

"No, sir. I dropped off the team, had to work on my grades."

"I remember watching you play football, couple of years ago. I watched a couple of games."

"Yes, sir, but you didn't come this last fall."

"No. You know why?"

We were all getting nervous, because Pa's voice was getting high, like it does when he's about to have a tirade or hit someone. So we all shut up.

"I asked, you know why?"

"Nossir."

"Because I saw you all afternoon blocking on the line, making big holes, and that nigger kid, the Tolliver kid, from over there outside of Powtown, those shanties there, he was running through those holes and making touchdowns. And after, all the newspapers could talk about was Tolliver, Tolliver. Never mentioned you one time."

I could've said something about how Billy Tolliver was so fast, you open a hole for him or you don't, doesn't matter, he's through there anyway. And he was the nicest running back I ever met, always come and give a high five to his linemen. I could've said, but when Pa gets going you shut up.

"Well, that Tolliver kid went to Auburn last year and, what do

The South Cornfield   55

you know, I never heard a word about him since, my son making blocks for him here and he gets the big head, everybody talking about him like he's the second coming of Christ, and he goes to Auburn and disappears, see what I mean?"

Ma was sitting there with her face all white, lips all tight, a sight we've seen a million times. I felt so sorry for her. Traxton or me or even Maryann could have told Pa that Billy Tolliver, when he got to Auburn, decided his name was Saleem Rasheed, and if you read the paper and looked for that name you'd see that he ran for more yards his freshman year than Bo Jackson did, so many years ago. But as I say, you don't interrupt Pa when he gets going.

"You go to State you'll just be blocking for niggers again, that's all." And his voice rose, although no one was arguing with him.

"Marlin—" Ma started to say. But he leaped up.

"And you're not going to play with niggers!" And he stormed out.

I had a bad night, not being hardly able to sleep, what with all the bad feelings about Pa. And then I woke up, the spring sun just beginning to come in my window. It was only six-thirty, and I could hear the tractor out there in the cornfield and I knew Pa was mad and taking it out on the cornfield. He was going to plow all the acreage he could so he wouldn't have to buy feed, same old story. I went back to sleep for a while, but when I woke up again and started to go downstairs I heard Maryann crying in her room. So I went in.

She didn't want to tell me anything, but then Traxton must've heard her too and there we all were, this little fifteen-year-old girl and her two big brothers—and we were big, I can tell you—both asking her what was wrong.

Well, she finally made up her mind and set her face and her voice like she wasn't going to cry anymore and she started.

"Pa came in my room last night, after we'd all been arguing and like that. And I was glad, because I hate it when he's mad at ever'one. And he was smiling a little and he sat down on the bed next to me and he told me, don't be worried. And then…he…then he opened my jammy tops and he…he touched me, you know, here? And then he suddenly got up and grabbed his face and he was crying. I never saw Pa cry before!"

And Traxton and me, we were staring at each other 'cause we couldn't imagine Pa crying either, and touching Maryann? Whoa!

"And then he just ran out of the room. And I couldn't sleep all night, and this morning I told Ma? And she slapped me one so hard across the face! Oh…Trax, Wally! I don't know what to do, what's going on! I'm scared."

Well, Trax got all red in the face, the first time I ever saw him really mad, and he said, "Come on, Wally, we got to talk to Ma!"

But when we got to the kitchen we saw Ma had all the pots and pans out and was washing them. That's what she'd do when she was real upset, pull everything out and wash it over and over again, and we knew we couldn't talk to her, so Traxton turns to me and says, "Wally, one time, we gotta have this out with Pa." And his face was set.

Well, that was a new one. Because Trax is the quiet one, a great big man who was much better at football than me in high school and a bunch of colleges wanted him, but Pa said he needed him to help run the farm and Trax never argued, and he's still here five years later. But now Trax was hot, and he stormed out of the house and I followed, wondering could Trax even face down our father, who everyone in the county was afraid of, the toughest guys hanging around the roadhouse with their pickups, even the sheriff.

We walked out along the dirt road, and halfway there we could hear the tractor wasn't running anymore, and we figured Pa was waiting for us, but when we crossed the rise we saw the furrows running all the way up on the bluff, but the tractor wasn't there and the old oak tree wasn't there and the end of Indian bluff wasn't there anymore, where it used to look out over the river.

ƒ

The South Cornfield

Things are going good this summer. Traxton is running the farm, and you'd never believe the change in Ma, how cheerful she can be now and then, although she's never going to be the jolliest woman you ever met. But she went to town with me the other day to buy me some new clothes for college, and I couldn't believe how she was, talking a mile a minute about styles and stuff. Maryann is seeing a counselor 'cause at first she thought it was all her fault, but now she says from what Ma remembers and from what she can figure out that Pa was always a hard man but then he just started getting nuts and that last night, with Maryann, that pushed him over the edge. And whether he just went too far with the tractor in his madness or if he finally saw that the end of the south cornfield was a good way out of his torment, we'll never know.

The Rabbit Farm

Julio began to worry about the offramp they'd taken twenty minutes or so after they'd crossed the George Washington Bridge. But it didn't bother him too much because Mrs. Shapiro had the map, after all. He was still cruising on a couple of tokes of the killer weed his pal Nigel had given him back at the garage before he took the bus to the school to pick up the kids. He figured the teacher, Mrs. Shapiro, would straighten it out. After all, he was only the bus driver, she was the boss, this was her class, and the kids were all happy in the back of the bus, singing some songs now. Only problem was, Mrs. Shapiro had been moaning the last half-hour about her bladder infection, and Julio wasn't sure she was paying attention to what was going on.

After leaving New York City you really get into some pure country in a hurry, the other side of the river, and Julio began looking around on those little roads for any kind of street sign, name of town, whatever, even if it wasn't his job. They were driving through

58

The Rabbit Farm

lanes of trees with turning leaves in the early fall—red, yellow, the kind everybody talked about. And then Mrs. Shapiro said this must be it, the third left, so he turned the bus and now the road was even narrower, dark, trees on all sides, and Julio would've suggested going back and asking someone, anyone—even behind that good dope he was getting worried—and then they saw the sign: MACDONALD'S RABBIT FARM.

The kids saw it too. They were third grade, after all; they spotted the sign as the bus slowed down, and they all cheered. They were all smart kids, from that private school up on Riverside Drive. Parents all tops in the professions. Julio liked the kids and drove the bus a lot for the school, even though it paid less than some other assignments. Little guys were funny, could joke with him, told him about vacations they took in places he never heard of. The kids were carrying on now,

"Old MacDonald had a farm, ee-aye ee-aye oh," and so forth.

Mrs. Shapiro had thought it was McDougall, or McDermott? McDermott's Bunny Farm and Petting Barn, a famous day trip for all the younger grades in Manhattan private schools. But at the moment she felt as if her urethra was transfixed by a red-hot needle. She was in agony, and when she saw the pleasant-faced middle-aged woman standing by the driveway and waving her hand, her only feeling was relief: this must be the place, finally. She forced herself to her feet as Julio opened the bus door.

"Hi, hi, hi! We're here!" she said, trying to sound half-way alive, bright, in control, a responsible teacher.

"Great! Sounds good!"

"Okay, kids! Out of the bus, we're at the farm!"

They needed no encouragement, scurrying down the bus steps, spreading in all directions, desperate for any kind of activity after an hour clustered in the yellow bus.

"You must be...uh, Mrs. McDermott?"

"Hi, hi. Yes. Great, great! Sounds good!" The woman came up, took both of Mrs. Shapiro's hands in hers. She had such a warm, friendly face, such trust.

"Mrs. McDermott, you'll have to forgive me but I've suddenly had an urgent attack of a…a problem with my bladder, and I'm going to go back to Paterson or somewhere with my driver, see if I can find a clinic. I hate to miss the orientation, but I should be back in an hour. Do you think you can handle the kids until then?"

"Great, great! Sounds good!" The woman's face lit up in an enthusiastic smile. Mrs. Shapiro was just barely able to wave at the children, yell to them, "Take care, now!" and then she was back in the bus, telling Julio, "Let's get out of here, back towards the bridge. There's got to be a walk-in clinic in Paterson somewhere, maybe before. We'll look in the phone book."

The bus drove off. The rollicking of the children gradually tapered off, and they started to mill around the nearest identifiable adult. As the pleasant woman at the edge of the driveway showed no sign of leading them off, or sign of anything, for that matter, Peter Maddy spoke to her. Peter was a leader—or a troublemaker, depending on the day of the week—but he always seemed to be able to grasp what was going on, even though he was one of the younger ones, at eight.

"So. When do we start the tour?" he asked the pleasant woman. She looked down at him, smiled, then turned back to the road as a car went by. She waved, said, "Hi, hi. Great! Sounds good!" She paid no more attention to the children.

Peter looked mildly puzzled, which wasn't normal for him, and Alexandra, who could sense any stray emotion wafting around, instantly seized his arm.

"What's the matter, Petey?"

"I don't know, I don't think this is Mrs. MacDonald, or something! Maybe—"

But at just that moment all the children saw a large man walking up the driveway. If they had been slightly worried about the place

The Rabbit Farm   61

they had been dropped—"dumped" was the word for it, said Bobby later—they were immediately reassured by the appearance of this man. This was a farmer. He was huge, larger than anyone's father, older too. He was wearing overalls and a blue work shirt, and he had a big tan cap on his head and hair growing out of his ears. At the moment he was smiling and trying to get the attention of the woman at the end of the driveway.

"Christina? What's going on here? Come on, child, time to go inside for a while."

The woman turned and obediently took his hand. He was looking around at the crowd of children—over twelve of them, near as he could tell. They started walking back to a complex of buildings nestled in the pines.

"Now, who can tell me what all of you are doing here?" he asked, still grinning. "I'm Mr. MacDonald."

"We're from the Walton Riverside School," said Peter, appointing himself the leader in this uncertain situation. "We have the day tour today." He looked around. "Mrs. Shapiro should be here, but I think she was sick."

"Her inside was burning," said Alexandra, dramatically. "That's what she was saying."

"Mrs. Shapiro?" said farmer MacDonald, his forehead creasing to indicate thought processes. "So Mrs. Shapiro would know what was going on?"

"We know too," said Leah Green. "We heard about it in class. We're going to see the bunnies and pet the animals." She gulped in embarrassment and tried to sink into the ground. Leah didn't like to talk out of turn.

"Well, Lord, you can sure look at the bunnies! Take all day if you want! Is this one of those County Mental Health things?" The children just looked at each other. Farmer MacDonald was thinking it over. "'Cause they were saying Christina needed more visitors and they were going to arrange something, I don't know."

Seeing the children's bewildered expression, he put on his cheerful smile again.

"That must be it. So you'll be Christina's visitors, and I'll show you all over the farm. I'm sorry. I must've missed a phone call from the county or something. Come on, let's go!"

"Why does Christina have to have visitors?" asked Bobby Kooper. Christina beamed when she heard her name spoken and waved to Bobby, saying, "Hi, hi. Sounds good!"

Farmer MacDonald put his arm around Christina, who immediately put her head against his shoulder and smiled sweetly at the children.

"Christina's my daughter. You see, she's simple. She's a big woman, you can see, forty years old, but inside her head she's your age, maybe even younger. But she's a good worker, aren't you, honey?"

"I'm a good worker, Daddy, sounds good!"

"So. We're all set! Let's go see the rabbits." But Christina interrupted. "Hot chocolate, Daddy! Time for hot chocolate!"

Farmer MacDonald stopped and looked back. "Darn, child! You're right! We should all have some hot chocolate. And maybe somebody needs to use the bathroom, too?"

With this, Farmer MacDonald won the hearts and minds of the Walton Riverside third grade. Some of the children had never had to feel anxiety about the availability of a bathroom before and were just beginning to feel the first pangs of urgency, perhaps influenced by Mrs. Shapiro's fairly explicit complaints all the way out there on the bus. So the pace picked up as they all walked towards the ancient, two-story frame house, grey and weather-stained.

Dr. Singh looked at Mrs. Shapiro gravely. She had managed to find an emergency clinic in the first town they'd come to, which to her surprise was Pompton Lakes rather than Paterson. Dr. Singh had taken her temperature and a urine specimen and then quickly took some blood and rushed into his lab. Now he was worried.

The Rabbit Farm   63

"Mrs. Shapiro, you have a temperature of one hundred and two degrees and your blood count is much too high. I worry that your bladder infection may reach your kidneys, and then you have problems!"

"But, Doctor, I have to get back to my kids, they're on a day trip and—"

"My receptionist will call your school to tell them the situation. I am sufficiently worried that I will drive you to the hospital myself. You are in risk of toxic shock, and the sooner the better. Nadine!" he called out the door, "I'm driving to Saint Luke's. Will you kindly take the information from Mrs. Shapiro's driver?"

And he bustled Mrs. Shapiro—protesting, but not very vigorously—out the door.

"What's going on? What was that all about?" Nadine asked Julio. She was a plump blond young woman, and they had been discussing a recent salsa special on MTV while the doctor was examining Mrs. Shapiro.

"Hey, ain't no big deal," said Julio. "I'll go back to the farm and wait for the kids. Coming out here, I know the roads now. Can I give you a call later, maybe? Could go dance some salsa, you know." He gave her a splendid smile and was out the door before Nadine remembered to ask for the phone number of the school.

It was Marla who picked up the phone at the Walton Riverside School. There was a breathy voice on the line.

"Hi. This is Antonia at the McDermott Bunny Farm. Did we get our wires crossed or something? I thought your third grade was coming in this morning?"

"Well, sure. They'll be there any—" and then Marla looked at the clock and saw the time, almost two hours late.

"Oh, my God!" she said. "They left here at eight-thirty! Our bus company is always—" And then she realized abruptly what she had to do. "I have to check immediately. I'll get back to you! Sorry about the—" And she hung up the phone.

Like all staff at the Walton Riverside School Marla knew the first thing she had to do was check to see just who the parents were of the children on board the missing bus. Third grade, let's see, here we are.

A. Buffington, that's Alexandra, of course. Father is...partner in Rentschler, Buffington, Schnee, brokerage, a Wall Street address. Not so good.

P. Maddy, son of Jane Maddy, separated from father P. Emerson Maddy, attorney.

E. Smith, um..um...no one important, thank God.

L. Green, that would be that dumb little daughter of...oh, my God...the U.S. ambassador to the United Nations. Ulp! Getting worse!

McF. Erickson, that's McFee—where do they get these names—daughter of the divorced wife of the Secretary of the Air Force? Jesus Christ!

And now R. Kooper, that would be Bobby, the little klutz, and he's the son of...the Attorney General of Connecticut.

Marla saw there were still eight names left, considered her options, including pretending she'd never taken the call and going out to lunch. But she knew that wouldn't work and that the prudent thing was just to pass off to higher authority. She pressed a button on her console.

"Mrs. Walton, I believe we have a problem here. Could I come see you for a moment?"

"Well, here's the rabbits," announced Farmer McDonald. "Some of 'em, anyway. We got two other sheds."

They were all standing inside a long roofed structure with only partial walls. Down each side was a long row of cages, four feet off the ground, and the children could see white creatures in every cage. Underneath the rows of cages was a long carpet of straw beginning to fill up with rabbit pellets. There was no mystery about the source of the pellets. The cage bottoms were of wire mesh, and the children

The Rabbit Farm

could see pellets falling from here and there, and now and then a flash of urine.

"These are the mommies," said Christina, proudly.

"That's right," said her father. "These are all breeding mothers, or about to be. You can see them charts on every cage, tell when they're going to have babies. The bigger young ones, they're all in the north shed. We let them run around together."

"Pee-you!" exclaimed Alexandra, who like all the others was amazed at the amount of excrement on the ground.

"Oh, pee-you, pee-you!" Some of the boys mocked her for her daintiness. "It's just rabbit poop," said Everett Chung.

"Rabbit poop! Of course that's what it is!" exclaimed Mr. MacDonald, and Christina giggled. "But you see, we're all organic here. We let all the poop and the pee fall on straw instead of on the ground. Rake it up every day, every pellet, and store it in that big composter over there by the woods. Come spring every year, there's better'n a ton in there."

"But what do you do with it?" asked Alexandra, making a face.

"Fertilizer," said Bobby. "They put it on plants."

"See! Is he a smart kid?" MacDonald said to his daughter. "Fertilizer is right! And the part what's worked down to the bottom gate is the best stuff in the world. It don't smell, and there's not a germ in it! We sack it and sell it all over the state. If you've ever eaten New Jersey strawberries, you've had a bit of MacDonald rabbit poop in there, somewhere."

The children were tickled pink at this choice nugget of information. They all giggled and nudged each other, and many of them began trying to imagine where they could first display their new knowledge.

A horn sounded, and a white refrigerator truck turned slowly down the gravel lane next to the sheds. A sign on the side identified it as Butler's Meats. Wholesale Restaurant Supply and Catering. A cheerful young redhaired man in white coveralls got out.

"Mornin', Mac! You got that order ready?"

"By golly, Billy! I forgot you were coming this morning! But the order's ready. We just gotta box it...." He looked around at the children.

"And we got some great little helpers here, don't we? You all want to help us load this gentleman's order?"

Few of the children had ever been asked to help do some real grown-up thing that working people did. So they all nodded eagerly and followed Mr. MacDonald to the end of the shed, where there was a big walk-in cold room.

MacDonald indicated a long stainless steel table just outside the entrance to the cold room.

"Christina, honey, you get the boxes ready there at the end. You kids, just line up along the table and we'll make a bucket brigade, just pass the little darlings along. Chris, she knows how to pack 'em just right."

And before the children could react here came the little skinned rabbit bodies, pink and scrunched up, cold and dry, and the children had to pass them along the line to Christina, who was unfolding waxed cardboard boxes with great concentration, her tongue sticking out of the left side of her mouth as she tried to remember which side of the box pulled out and where the slots fitted.

Farmer MacDonald kept talking, which helped keep the more horrified children from thinking about what they were handling.

"Half the rabbit you're going to eat in a New York restaurant comes from here. They know they can count on MacDonald rabbit. You know, years ago, they had laws, you had to leave the rabbit's head and paws on, so customers would know it was a rabbit instead of a cat."

"A cat?" blurted Leah, in spite of herself. "Eat a kitty?"

"Well, of course, no one wants to eat a kitty, that's the whole point. But back when I was your age, we were real poor down there in Newark, lots of people were really poor, and if you could catch a

The Rabbit Farm   67

poor cat in an alley and kill it and skin it, cut the head and the paws off, it wasn't that hard to pass it off as a rabbit, maybe make forty cents or so. Not very good eating, I should say. Tasted part of one once."

"You ate a kitty?" This from Bobby. There was dead silence from the other children.

"Didn't mean to. My sis went to the market instead of Mom. Mom was sick, actually dying then, though we didn't know."

MacDonald gave sort of a rueful chuckle and shook his head, as if just thinking about all those jokes life could play on you.

"Sis thought she was buying a rabbit at a real good price. Those days we'd put a rabbit, or a chicken if we were lucky, in the pot, a lot of onions and water, and boil it up. Potatoes too, if we had one or two left. Turnips sometimes. They were real cheap, but we were sick of them. Whole thing was to stretch everything out so all five of us could eat something. Momma was in bed, and she was hungry. She was eating her meat and potatoes and soup out of the bowl, but Pa, at the kitchen table, he put his spoon down. Time Momma got through he went and took her bowl and kissed her, told her to go back to sleep. Then he closed her door, came back in the kitchen, and told us in a soft voice, 'Mother needed her food, so I didn't say nothin'. But that was a cat we put in the pot. I can't eat it, and you don't have to either.' Well we all knew something was wrong with that taste, so that night we all went hungry. And now we're all done! All the little guys packed away! We couldn't have done it without you, could we, Christina?"

"That's right, Daddy! Great, great! Sounds good!"

The meat truck had gone, Farmer MacDonald let all the children wash their hands at the faucet, and then Esmé Smith, against all odds, was the one who asked the question uppermost in all minds.

"Mr. MacDonald? Who kills the bunnies?"

The farmer bent over to look closely at the little girl, a colorless girl who could get lost in a crowd—wispy light brown hair, a sort of heavy face and lumpy body, but right now, very intense eyes, dark brown eyes.

"Well, honey, we have to kill them. They're our friends, we raise them up, feed 'em, and all, and there's only one reason we raise 'em. So someone can eat them. So we don't like to do it, but we do it. Doesn't hurt them a bit, they don't know it even happened."

"How do you kill them?" asked Peter Maddy.

"We gotta do a dozen or so today." MacDonald looked doubtful. "You sure you're supposed to see all this?"

Half the children were goggle-eyed and silent, mouths open. The other half, mostly the boys, immediately responded.

"Oh, yes! We're supposed to see everything!"

"Well...okay. Christina, let's go over to the next shed and start on that batch."

There was an ominous machine on a bench. Christina brought a rabbit out of a big hutch full of young rabbits running around.

"Old Chris! She's great with the young ones! They come right up to her fingers when she wiggles them. She can pick 'em right up, not scared at all. Now we just take this little guy—and you know, all rabbits like to go into holes, so we put his little head through here, he starts to stretch out, and...."

The machine made a click and Farmer MacDonald brought back the twitching body of the rabbit, missing its head and bleeding furiously at the neck. One glance at the faces of his audience was enough for him to decide that perhaps they weren't supposed to see everything. Only Peter Maddy ducked around the other side of the machine to see where the head had gone.

"Christina, honey. It's getting along to be lunchtime. Why don't you take your friends into the kitchen for some lunch? I think we'll fry up that bag of rabbit wings."

This was a fortunate phrase. The image of the headless rabbit was driven from the children's minds by the mention of rabbit wings.

The Rabbit Farm

"Uh, Christina," asked Alexandra, as they were walking up to the house. "Did your father say rabbit wings?"

"Rabbits don't have wings!" exclaimed Everett Chung. Some of the girls giggled, and Bobby Kooper flapped his arms.

"They're the best part," said Christina, calmly. "You wait and see."

The mystery was solved when farmer MacDonald rejoined them in the large kitchen, where Christina had set out a big metal bowl and was now taking a plastic bag out of the refrigerator.

"They're just the little front legs. We call 'em wings 'cause they're like chicken wings. Bony and hard to eat, but they got the most flavor. Sometimes the restaurants only want the thighs and saddle. So we keep the wings, eat 'em all the time."

Jane Maddy picked up the phone.

"It's me, babe. What's it look like for tonight?"

"Oh! Mario! God! Thank God you called! I've been going crazy! The school called about an hour ago and said the bus never showed up at the...uh...whatever, wherever the kids were going today on this day trip. They said, 'Don't worry,' but Jesus! How can I not—"

"Where was Peter going?"

"Oh, some goddamn farm in New Jersey. They were going to pet rabbits or something. Now, stop laughing! It's serious!"

"Hey, Janey, it's just a mixup of some kind. Kids at that school have such important families, something like this happens, everybody starts thinking, 'Hostage situation!'"

"Well, it could be...."

"Come on babe! Listen, I'll make some phone calls, find out if the feds or anybody is alerted. I'll let you—"

"Oh, God! If you would, Mario."

"Count on it! Now, here's the picture: I got a serious final permit hearing this afternoon. About forty acres for a mall in south Jersey.

It's going to be a dogfight, all your environmentalists out there as usual. I get through with that I'd like to get out of the combat zone and relax for a while. Petey gets home okay, what's tonight look like?"

"God! I'd love to see you! Petey will too!"

Mario chuckled. "I dunno, babe. I don't think your kid's warmed up to me yet, last couple of times I was over."

"Mario! Come on! Just 'cause he called you 'Godfather?' He saw the video over at Alexandra's house last week, and I don't know how her crazy parents can let her watch stuff like that. You're the only Italian he knows!"

"American, American, babe! Third generation? MBA from Dartmouth? How WASP can you get? Look, I gotta run. Just remember, no hostage situation!"

"It's very possibly a hostage situation," said the Director of the FBI. He was on the phone to the secretary of the Air Force, who had just called him again in a panic. "I've called the top state police people in New Jersey, and they're trying to get organized, but in that corner of New Jersey, up there by the border, there're about forty little jurisdictions, one-cop towns, you know what I mean?"

"My wife is going crazy! My ex-wife, that is. She's blaming it all on me, thinks I'm the target!"

"Mac, it's hard to say. I got the list of parents from the school the first time you called, and we have three, maybe four parents, net worth up there in the mid-eight figures, couple others like you with national security exposure. We can't figure out who's the target. I'll keep in touch. Is there anything you can be doing?"

"Right now? I gotta tell you off the record, Fred, but I scrambled a U2 out of McGuire soon as I heard, and the guy's up there now plotting every yellow bus in northern New Jersey on a computer map. He thinks it's a training problem."

"That's super, Mac. We get the reports on the normal local

The Rabbit Farm   71

school bus traffic, the computer should spot the odd one right away!
Okay! I'll be in close touch!"

After an hour of frustrated driving on country roads, Julio finally
saw a familiar turnoff. A few minutes later he turned into the
MacDonald farm driveway and parked under some big trees. He'd
stopped for a large lunch at a burger joint on the highway and
thought he'd be safe taking a little nap. He couldn't see the kids anywhere; they must be on the tour or whatever it was. So he went back
to the long back seat and turned in.

The little rabbit wings were popping around beautifully in the big
fat fryer. The children were enthusiastically dredging the last raw
ones in flour and seasonings in the big bowl, shaking them off and
passing them for Christina to put in the fat.

"Best thing to go with that is good farm bread and some cole
slaw," said Farmer MacDonald. He was passing cabbage heads over
a shredder into a bowl with a puddle of lemon juice, olive oil, and
mayonnaise on the bottom. "The slaw here cuts the grease."

A few moments later the children sat down around the big
kitchen table. A few chairs from the living room and study had been
dragged in to make up the number. There was a steaming pile of
golden rabbit wings on a huge platter, a bowl of cole slaw, and a bas-
ket of bread.

"Christina, bring some forks for the slaw, honey." He explained
to the children, "You gotta have a fork for the slaw, but you just grab
those legs at the end and chew 'em like corn on the cob. Who wants
ketchup?"

"Mr. MacDonald?" This was Leah Green.

"Yes, sweetie? What do you need?"

"I don't think rabbit is kosher. Maybe I shouldn't eat it."

Bobby Kooper laughed. "My folks are Jewish too, Leah. And I
was at your birthday party when we had Chinese, remember?

Nobody cared about kosher then! Your mother was joking about it!"

Esmé Smith put up her hand and spoke almost soundlessly. "Mr. MacDonald? I have to eat kosher too."

The big man beamed. "Well, there's nothing simpler, honey! Christina! Whyn't you make a big plate of peanut butter and jelly sandwiches? Anyone doesn't want to eat rabbit can have one of them."

A few minutes later nothing could be heard but the sounds of eating.

The director of the FBI was on a conference call with the mayor of New York, the police commissioner, the deputy commander of the New Jersey State Police, Mrs. Ashley Walton of the Walton Riverside School, and six of the concerned parents.

"Let me get this straight," said the director. "No one here, no one at all has received a ransom demand, no message of any kind?"

The answer was an agonized negative.

"My God!" cried Mrs. Buffington. "It'd almost be better if we knew someone had them. Safe, I mean. But not knowing…" and she began crying again.

"Well, then. This is a puzzle," said the director. "We have every agency in New Jersey out scouring the roads. We talked to the bus company. The manager says this guy Julio Villegas has been driving for them five years, no problems, good man, good attitude, very dependable."

"Vee-yay-goss," said Mr. Buffington, pronouncing it the way he'd heard it, "What kind of name is that?"

"I have no idea," said Mrs. Walton, bristling a little. "He's an American citizen and has a high school diploma here in New York. That's all the bus company requires."

"But it could be a Cuban name," said the police commissioner, "and if we find out this is a Castro operation, I'm going to…."

The Rabbit Farm   73

There were agonized cries from three of the mothers on the line.

"Let's try to be rational about this," said the mayor. "We have no reason to believe there's even been a kidnapping, let alone some kind of weird foreign plot. We could just be dealing with a lost bus!"

Mr. Buffington immediately realized that his importance in this situation was being threatened, and he responded with some heat.

"Well! In that case let me tell you that I am authorizing my law firm to start a suit for child endangerment in the amount of one hundred million dollars against, jointly, the Walton School and the City of New York for inadequate licensing regulations!"

The amount caught the fancy of several of the parents, and they chimed in that they would join the suit. The FBI director, although realizing that he had originally mentioned the magic word, "hostage," thought it was time to reassert control.

"Ladies and gentlemen, I don't think we should let our imaginations run wild here. Let me assure you that our people are covering every eventuality and that they will contact you the second we have hard information." And he closed the line in the midst of clamoring interruptions.

"Well, we don't have too many other animals, but I can show you our pigs, Mama and her little ones. But I don't know about petting...."

After lunch several of the children had asked Farmer MacDonald about the petting barn they had been told about. It turned out that he had no baby ducks, or lambs, or goats, and only two cows, who were out in a back pasture and tended to be antisocial.

They approached a large enclosure surrounded by a wall built of massive old railroad ties. Half of the enclosure was covered by a makeshift shingled roof, but the mother pig and her children were out in the sunny part, as it was a chilly day. The sow was huge, and her tiny red eyes shifted back and forth between her little piglets dashing around and the visitors now clustering around the top row of railroad ties. Not even the most naïve, romantic child believed that her rather calculating expression was an invitation to be petted.

"Now, all of you be careful! Pigs aren't much for petting, anyway. And if anyone fell in that pen they might wind up like old Barlow's dogs!"

"Who are Barlow's dogs?" asked Peter Maddy immediately.

Farmer MacDonald pointed to what the children had thought were two rugs hanging from an oak branch. One was black, the other sort of yellow.

"I warned Barlow a bunch of times not to let his dogs come over here. They killed a couple of my chickens and they were always trying to get into the rabbit hutches. They'd run around the big hutch there where the young rabbits all are, scare 'em to death, get 'em dashing around, a couple of times some of the little guys got crazy and killed themselves running into the wire."

The children were agog at this tale of dog misbehavior.

"So I told Barlow that my sow was having little ones and he should watch his dogs. He just badmouthed me as usual, and one morning we came out here, me and Christina, and both dogs were on the bottom of the pen, just the way you see them hanging there. Flat. They'd jumped down into the pen to get at the little ones, and old Flossie just chased them, squashed them up against the side of the pen and then tromped them flat. She's four hundred pounds if she's an ounce. She looks heavy and slow but she can move like lightning! She ate about half of 'em, too, the soft parts. I called Barlow and told him he could come and get his dogs back if he needed a couple throw rugs." He chuckled, and some of the children laughed uneasily too.

"You just don't want to mess with a mean pig, you know what I mean? Come on, let's go back up and check out the rabbits."

"Mr. MacDonald?" asked McFee Erickson. "If you keep, uh, killing the bunnies and selling them, how do you get new ones?"

The Rabbit Farm 75

MacDonald looked at Christina and they both laughed.

"We never have to worry about that, do we honey? We got some real bunny factories here. Chris? Do you think it's old Annie's time again?"

"'Bout a month, Daddy. Sounds good!"

They were all entering the third building. On one side were single hutches. On the other, a few cages with large rabbits in them and several empty cages.

"Okay," said MacDonald, "We're going to put Butch, here, in what we call the honeymoon hotel." And he picked up a large gray-and-white rabbit from one cage and put him in an empty one.

"Now we get Annie, here, and put her in with Butch."

The children had never watched anything with such rapt attention. They were as sure as anything in the world that what they were watching was forbidden. Butch and Annie ran around the cage a couple of times. Then Butch came up and sniffed Annie's behind. She ran off, let Butch catch up, ran off again, repeated this maneuver three times. Then suddenly they ran as fast as they could around the cage. Just as suddenly Annie stopped, raised her rump in the air. Butch was on her in a second, bounced up and down a few times, shrieked, and fell twitching to the floor of the cage. Annie wandered off aimlessly and began chewing at a bit of celery that had been left in the cage.

"The bunnies are fucking!" said Christina, giggling. The children looked at her with wonder. All of them knew that she'd said a bad word.

"Well, that's strong language, Christina," said her father, chuckling a bit and patting her on the shoulder. He was looking around at the children, smiling and sort of shaking his head. "We like to say they're 'romancing.' Anyway. About a month from now Annie's going to have a litter. Twenty-nine days, thirty days, usually. Now come along here and I'll show you. See this cage? Betsy's about two days from having her little babies. See? She's pulled a lot of fur out of her chest and put it in that box full of straw, just getting ready to keep her young ones warm. Now, over here is Jackie, just had her babies five days ago."

The children could see the rabbit lying on its side in the nest of fur, with five tiny, hairless, blind babies rooting at her nipples.

"And over here is Susie and her kids. One of them died, but the rest are real healthy and ready to go in the big pen." The children could see a large, lethargic mother surrounded by very active baby rabbits the size of a child's hand, all rushing around, carrying on, trying to unearth their mother's nipples, which she was carefully lying firmly on top of.

"So. That's the story of rabbits! You saw the young ones, you saw them grow up, go on to be our dinner, you saw the bunnies making new bunnies, you saw the whole picture! You even had some rabbit wings for lunch! You got any questions, or maybe it's time for you to go on back home?"

Farmer MacDonald had spotted Julio, now woken up from his nap, strolling casually back into the yard and waving at the children. It was three o'clock.

Mrs. Walton answered the door and let in a flood of parents.

"Yes, yes, hello, hello, Mrs. Buffington, Mr. Chung, yes. Hello, Rabbi Smith. All of you! Please go into the reception. We've got a TV set up in there, and we've got our switchboard on direct to the FBI and the Mayor's office. This is Agent Hameed from the FBI, and over there is Lieutenant O'Brien from the police." Agent Hameed was huge and black, and he did not smile back at the parents.

The parents had all seen innumerable African-Americans playing FBI agents in movies and television dramas, but they were not reassured to see a black man with an Arab name in charge of the crisis in which their children were involved. Lieutenant O'Brien was large himself, but old, red-faced, fat. He grinned awkwardly, waved a hand, and said, "Harya doin'?" The old New Yorkers in the crowd

The Rabbit Farm   77

sighed. They were certain that if there was a hostage situation it would not be resolved by an old doughnut snarfer like O'Brien.

"Oh, my God!" said Mrs. Walton, looking out the window. Just pulling into the street in front of the Walton-Riverside School was a big television van. As the parents clustered at the window another van pulled up across the street. Crews piled out of the vans and started setting up their cameras. A tall young man with wavy hair began combing his hair while looking at a script, and on the other side of the street they could see a hard-faced young woman checking her makeup in a mirror held by an assistant.

"What the hell is going on?" demanded Mrs. Green.

The bus was on its way back through the wooded countryside of northern New Jersey. The children were still singing "Old MacDonald had a farm" and were making up sounds that rabbits made while "romancing," or dogs being stepped on by pigs, giggling and getting a little disorderly, saying, "Sounds good! Sounds good!" in imitation of Christina. Some of them were repeating what Christina had said about the rabbits romancing until it didn't even sound like a bad word anymore. They were all still enchanted by their day and rehearsing in their minds all the wonders they would describe to their parents. Peter Maddy was sitting next to Alexandra Buffington.

"If I show you something, can you keep a secret?" he asked.

She looked at him skeptically. Everyone knew Peter was a piece of work.

"What? And where is it?" she finally asked.

Peter opened his little fanny pack slowly. "Ta da!"

As Alexandra started to scream he grabbed her and put his mouth right next to her ear. "You promised!" he hissed.

Alexandra was looking at a rabbit head. Its eyes were open, and it looked completely alive, calm, looking out of the pack as if it had always lived there.

"I picked it up from behind that machine, you know? The one that cuts the heads off? I'm going to take it home and play a trick!" Peter giggled.

"Petey! You're terrible! You're going to get in trouble! What kind of trick?"

"I can't say just yet. I'll tell you tomorrow. But *no telling*, you hear me?" He whispered insistently.

"I don't want to know! I think you're disgusting!" she hissed back.

"Hey, kids," said Julio, turning around and shouting back into the back of the bus. "I think we got a police escort or something!"

At the Air Force base a woman with her eyes glued to a computer screen was talking to the U2 pilot in the air over New Jersey.

"Are you sure that's the one you're looking for?" asked the pilot.

"That's the one that's not accounted for by the local traffic," she responded. "And it's headed back towards the George Washington Bridge. We just put local ground forces on it, New Jersey state troopers."

"So what's this all about?" asked the pilot. "Is this an exercise, or what?"

"That's classified, Captain," said the woman. "Stand by to return to base."

"They're in heavy turnpike traffic," said the state trooper to his radio audience, which included the director of the FBI, the secretary of the Air Force, the mayor of New York, and a dozen other public law enforcement agencies, as well as the link to the parents at the Walton Riverside School.

"I don't think I should pull them over. They seem to be headed back to the school."

"Can you see any obvious terrorists controlling the bus?" asked the FBI director.

The Rabbit Farm   79

"No. In fact, the kids all seem to be clustered in the back of the bus waving at me. Are we sure there's a hostage situation here?"

As the bus crossed over the George Washington Bridge and took the winding offramps onto Manhattan streets it was joined by five NYPD cars, gumballs flashing, escorting it down Riverside Drive. At one corner two dark blue sedans pulled out in front of the bus, and an arm from the first one waved to Julio, "Follow me!"

"Jeez! I don't know what's going on here!" said Julio. "Any you kids got any idea? We on the wrong street or something?"

The children stared at their escorts with wonder. But as the bus slowed, turned the corner, and came slowly down the block to their school, they could all see a crowd in front, television cameras…and there were some of their parents, waving frantically.

"Whoa!" said Peter Maddy, "Something's going on!" But the other children were delighted to see their mothers, their fathers, all gathered to welcome them.

The doors of the bus opened. The television cameras focused. There was a hush for a moment. Then little Esmé Smith, the quiet child, burst out of the bus, waving to her mother.

"Mommy, Mommy, we saw bunnies fucking!"

"Jesus, I wish this was live," said one cameraman under his breath.

"We ate rabbit wings!"

"Farmer MacDonald cut the bunny heads off in a machine!"

"His daughter's simple!"

"We helped her pack the dead bunnies!"

"His mother ate a cat and died!"

"There's bunny poop in our strawberries!"

"His pig squished two dogs!"

"And ate them, too!

The joyous news went on and on, recorded by four different television channels until the reporters, disgusted that there was no real story except a trip to the wrong rabbit farm, started packing up to leave. The cameramen all knew the parts of the footage that were going to make the all-time outtake file.

"Petey get to sleep okay?" asked Mario, coming up the stairs. Jane Maddy was standing at the top in her nightgown, a big smile on her face.

"He babbled all about today for about an hour. I thought he'd never run down. But he's out like a light. Must have been a big day for him!"

"You too, babe! You okay, no stress anymore?"

"No, no, not at all. You can't believe the relief we all felt. And then the parents' faces when the kids started yelling these unbelievable things. I was laughing so hard I thought I'd pee in my pants. I'll tell you the best parts when we get to bed."

A few moments later Mario emerged from the steamy bathroom, naked except for the towel around his waist. Jane was standing by the bed looking naughty.

"God, it's great to be here! After my afternoon, too!" said Mario. "I'll tell you later." And that was when he threw the covers back.

Timmy's in the Well

The dog started barking again around six, just when she'd poured herself a drink and sat down at the computer. It wasn't a normal *arf-arf*, he had a nervewracking scraping kind of yelp, fingernails on the blackboard, that kind of bark. Julia tried to keep working on her article, but it was no use. She got up and yelled down the stairs, "Danny! He's driving me crazy! Go over there again, and this time...."

But something in the echo of her voice told her that Dan wasn't there. He must have gone down to the village butcher's to get dinner. She looked at her watch. Sixish. That was about normal if they didn't have leftovers to eat. He was going to cook something for dinner.

Dan had gotten a good contract for his proposed *Cooking in Provence* and they were over here in an eighteenth-century stone house built into the medieval wall of a little farm village in the hills east of Avignon. His publisher knew the owner, who never used it.

Dan had four good-selling cookbooks, and he could have easily written this at home in Connecticut but he wanted the atmosphere and to be able to buy good French food and cook it here in Provence. Julia had her own writing to do and was about to stay home, but her publisher told her, no problem, we'll pay for a fax there in France, just keep sending the pages, we're all one electronic world now. So she'd been doing well on the three contracted articles—except for the damned dog.

Dan had a theory about the barking dogs. "Every family in France has a dog," he'd said. "You have to get used to it. In the evening the first guy who gets home feeds his dog. All the other dogs a mile around can smell what's happening and they want to be fed too. So they bark. Listen," he said, waving down her objections "You know Jeannot, over there across the court? Works at the Total station out on the D 32? He starts work at seven, so he comes home around five or so after a few drinks at the café. He's home first, so he calls that idiot boxer of his in his high voice...." Dan pursed his lips, sounded, "Qui-*nou*, Qui-*nou*," almost like a bird call. Julia had to laugh, it was perfect. Dan went on, "Watch, I'll show you." And he went outside on the upstairs terrace and started calling, "Qui-*nou*, Qui-*nou*!" Immediately four dogs started barking in the neighborhood, and the yelping of the dog next door was like an icepick in Julia's ears.

"Danny! Stop it...it drives me nuts!"

"So, I tell you what. When the dogs start barking everyday, late afternoon, we'll walk into the village, drink a pastis, talk to the locals, and catch up on the town gossip. All the monsters get fed, we'll come home and we can both work for a while before dinner. Okay?"

She'd said it was okay, but it wasn't. For some weird reason she didn't usually like writing in the morning. But four or five o'clock in the afternoon, first drink of the day, she was charged. She could write seven or eight pages, hearing Dan cooking dinner downstairs, refreshing her drink now and then, coming down around eight,

Timmy's in the Well   83

eight-thirty, really happy with what she'd written, knowing she
could clean it up in the morning easily with that new word process-
ing program she'd put on the old Mac. But the problem was that in
late afternoon the dogs started, and the next door neighbor's was the
worst. The yelper. A widow lived there and never fed her dog until
dark. So there were about two, two-and-a-half hours of barking,
that awful yelp that made it impossible to concentrate.

Dan had gone over to talk to Madame Flacelière, but his French
wasn't very good and Madame was old and vague, purposely misunderstanding: *It is so difficult, my children want me to go to a home. I
have so much to do, I must have a dog barking against the thieves, they
rob every house these days....* Julia went over one day, out of her mind
from the barking, wanting to see the awful creature making this
noise. She'd expected to see one of the German killer dogs the
French all seemed to love, or a neurotic little yapmeister. Instead it
turned out to be a sweet-faced smallish dog, sort of reddish, long-
haired, intelligent-looking and immediately focusing on her there
over the fence with a frown of worry, seeming to ask her, who's going to feed me, take care of me? Having seen the widow Flacelière
tottering around, Julia had to admit that the dog had a point. She
was sure that many times Madame Flacelière had simply forgotten
to feed her dog in the evening.

She heard Dan coming in downstairs. "Honey, I'm home!" he
yelled, in his eternal parody of some old TV series. He'd been doing
it for five years now, and she still found it funny when she was in a
good mood, but the rest of the time she wanted to throw a pan of
food in his face, if he liked old comedy that much. Trouble was, he
was the cook—he was the guy with the pans of food, which she
hardly ever touched. He did all the cooking, even all the cleaning up,
if you could believe it. Julia went downstairs, still hearing the
"*Yelp...yelp...yelp...*" from next door, just like clockwork.

"Dan, I'm really going crazy. And I thought I'd finish the travel
article tonight. Can you go talk to that hag again? She'll listen to you."

Dan was shaking his head in sympathy, smiling. "It's awful, babe! I'm going right over there."

She loved him so much, he always knew what she really wanted, never gave her one of those we-men-know-what's-best kind of arguments. She felt a little misty, watching him stride next door, tan legs in his shorts, good bod, even eating all the great French food he cooked. She had her hands on her hips and couldn't help feeling to see if she was putting on inches. She knew she was. The scale told her.

A few minutes later the barking stopped, but Dan didn't come back for a bit. When he did he looked serious.

"The ambulance came for Madame today. She thought she was having a heart attack, I talked to her niece, you know, Monique? Had to come over from Mazan? Madame's in the hospital in Carpentras, and they say she's resting okay now. Anyway, we fed the dog for tonight."

"Oh, God! That dog! The poor thing! I feel so guilty, it has such a sweet face. How can it make that awful sound? I was going out of my mind!"

"Well, I told Monique we'd feed the dog for a few days, however long it takes. Maybe if we had it over here, in our yard, played with it or something, it wouldn't feel so helpless, like it had to bark all the time. You know?"

Julia knew she had no talent for playing with dogs, and she thought it was a bad idea. "I'll go over and feed it. At least it won't have these anxiety attacks, for Christ's sake!"

"You remember," Dan said, "I have to go up to Mondragon tomorrow to review that restaurant. You know what French lunches are like. I probably won't be back till five or so. Sure you don't want to come?"

Julia always felt out of sorts when he asked her these questions. The problem was they were in maybe the biggest meat-eating country in the world and she was practically a vegetarian, maybe a little piece of salmon now and then. But she hid her irritation and nodded.

Timmy's in the Well   85

"I remembered. You just go and have fun. I'll keep an eye on the dog, feed it if it gets hungry. I could finish two assignments if I could work steady. What's the little asshole's name?" She had realized, guiltily, that she was calling the dog "it" and didn't even know its gender.

So the next morning, after Dan left, Julia went over and fed little Robert (Ro-*bair*, as the French said). She patted him and scratched his ears, and he wiggled his behind and smiled, so she figured she could leave him alone. Then it was great in the morning for once. Her ideas were flowing, and she finished her article and was most of the way through the second. She felt so good about it that she called her agent in New York, woke him up at seven in the morning and talked to him for an hour. Then it was past noon and she was getting hungry. Little Robert hadn't made a sound for an hour and she figured he was asleep, so she went down into the village for a salad at the Café du Cours. She ran into the Wilders there and had a hilarious conversation about the mayor's sexy wife, who everyone knew was having it on with the *entraineur* of the local rugby team, a tall, slim, long-haired dreamboat. Back at the house the work continued well, but then she seemed to hear a dog barking again. Ro*bair*! She'd forgotten all about him and went clumping down the stairs and out into the yard.

In their part of the village the backyards sloped downhill into the fields and vineyards. They faced west, and in the afternoon the sun could be much too bright and hot, reflecting white off the surrounding dusty fields. Years ago the crops had all depended on wells, but now they had irrigation and the old wells skulked at the lower corners of the fields. She could just barely hear the yelping now, so she walked across the little alley and let herself into Madame Flacelière's yard. No little dog came rushing to greet her so she stopped and stood completely still for a moment. After a bit she could hear the yelping again, weak sounding, and it seemed to be outside the yard, sounded like down in the vineyard, and she thought, *The little monster is chasing a cat or something. How the hell did he get out?*

She walked downhill, following the last sound she'd heard of that familiar barking. There was a dirt path going around the vineyard, and she paused there, listening. Then there was a yelp quite near, funny sounding, with a weird echo. Julia looked around. In the afternoon sun the world was still in heat and brightness. Above her the village of St. Gens shimmered in the heat, but nothing moved, everyone seeking a nap in the shadiest rooms of their houses. The town looked like one of those dead villages up in the hills where no one had lived for fifty years.

She tried calling. "Ro-*bair*! Ro-*bair*!" *Where the hell are you, you little bastard!* Then there was another muffled yelp, almost gargled, and suddenly she focused on the low stone well to the east. Jesus! Was he in the well? She ran over, saw the rotten wooden cover that someone had pulled partly aside. She tried to look down, but it was too dark. She was rewarded, however, with a passionate yelp from below. Christ! Robert was in the well! Struggling, cursing, she managed to push the cover mostly off the well head. There below was the little dog, grimly paddling in the murk. He gave another soft yelp and then sank under the surface of the water for a second, evidently from the exertion of calling.

The poor little guy! Julia looked frantically around for some man. Then she wondered if she should run up into the village and try to find someone awake. Would they all laugh at her? She had no confidence in a French village. She'd never felt close to anyone here, they all seemed so distant, preferring to talk to Dan, although her French was much better than his. *Well, the hell with French men*, was her reaction. *Timmy's in the well! I don't have to send Lassie for help, or whatever.* Attached to the side of the well was a sturdy wooden post that had once been part of the superstructure. There was an old rope looped around it, obviously part of the old pulley mechanism that had been removed years before. And there were two mossy old wooden steps that had been bolted to the stones on the side of the well God knew how long ago.

Timmy's in the Well

Julia thought rapidly. She had climbed mountains. She knew how to rappel down rock faces. She'd written an article about it for *Sunset*. She'd go down and save the dog, get him on her shoulders or something, then just pull her way back up again. What could it be down there, ten feet? Piece of cake!

The well face was made of mortared stones, which made it easy for her to grab the rope and begin to lower herself down, toehold by toehold. Halfway down the well face had been mortared over, but the surface was still rough enough for her sandals to get a purchase and the last old piece of wood was right at water's edge. That was when she began to wonder, *why did I come down here in my sandals. At least I've only got on shorts and a halter. But I could have changed to my running shoes! Oh well. Too late now.*

The water was almost a relief when she entered it after struggling down in the afternoon heat. It wasn't even cool, it was just plain cold, rising from the limestone below, fed by melting Alpine snows a hundred kilometers away. She knew, she'd written a story about the Fontaine de Vaucluse over the next hill. But she forgot all these thoughts at the relief of being able to hold the rope with one hand and support the feeble little body of Robert with her other arm. The poor little bastard! He felt so weak! He must have been paddling down here for three hours or more. She could see his front paws, torn from trying to get a clawhold on the rough mortar, bleeding down her arm now as he tried to lick her face in pathetic gratitude.

"How the hell did you get down here, you little asshole?" she asked. "Did you chase a rat or something under the cover?" He whined softly.

"Okay, pal, now we're going back up. And you have to cooperate." She managed to get him around to where he could ride piggyback, his forepaws over her shoulders. He was trembling from the cold, but he seemed to know what was needed, could sense the procedure.

"Okay, Ro-*bair*, here we go," and she gripped the rope hard and began to walk her way up the wall. For a second she was worried that she might not have the strength, with an extra what—twenty pounds?—on her back. But then she thought, *I've done this with even a heavier pack on*, and she concentrated on the muscles she was using: keep it slow, nice and easy, hand over hand, a few inches at a time, keep the feet firmly planted.

As her hands reached up into the sunlight slanting down into the well she could feel Robert tensing against her back, and she thought, *Oh great! He's going to leap up over me. Probably scratch the shit out of my back and knock me back into the well!* So she took an extra firm grip with both hands and pulled hard, getting ready.

The rotten rope suddenly gave way, and they both plunged back into the well, Julia striking her head a glancing blow on the side of the shaft as she fell. Everything went black.

Julia's eyes opened and saw a wall. She was back in her house looking at the century-old stone wall of their bedroom. *It was a dream!* she thought. *God! What a terrible dream!* And then water entered her nose and she realized it wasn't a dream, she was back in the well.

She thrashed about for a few seconds before she was completely conscious again. And then she was pushed under one more time by little Robert trying to climb on her back. Sputtering, cursing, she kicked her way back up, treaded water, made Robert cling to her arm instead of climbing on her back. She looked around. There was that piece of wood. Could she climb up on that? But it was slimy with moss, and without a rope to hold onto it would be impossible to pull herself up. Then she wondered, *How deep is this well? Maybe there's a bottom somewhere I could stand on.*

So she told little Robert, "just hang in there a minute, buddy," took a breath and let herself sink down. Whoops. Out of luck! She didn't hit anything for about four feet, and then it was some rusty machinery that someone had thrown in there and she was terrified of being caught in it and came scrambling and sputtering again to

Timmy's in the Well   89

the surface to be mounted again by an almost hysterical Robert, whimpering and clawing.

So. She and Robert were going to have to wait until someone came by and heard her call. And when would that be? She thought of St. Gens asleep in the afternoon heat. When did anyone come out? There were workers in the vineyard, Arabs who could be seen in the morning but who also disappeared in the afternoon. She might have to wait until late afternoon. The once refreshing water was now quite cold, and she began to worry, *Can I last a few hours in water this cold? Will my fingers still be able to hold on to this slimy board?*

As she was thinking she suddenly heard the voices of children. Of course! Kids sometimes walked by here in the afternoon, it was a shortcut from the upper end of town to…where? Somewhere! She'd seen them before from the upstairs window. She'd just give them a call.

But nothing came out but an asthmatic croak. Her throat had swollen, as it often did under stress. Try as she would, she could not make a sound that would carry out of her throat. In frustration she tried to scream at Robert, but it came out a hoarse whisper, "Bark! bark! you little fucker!" desperately willing him to start up his famous yelp. But Robert only nodded his head, smiling at her in a worried way, knowing that she, the big human, could handle this problem. He wouldn't make a sound. So she went crazy, trying to scream, splashing the water, cursing the stupid, senseless little kids going by, until she heard gargling and realized that she'd scared the shit out of Robert, that he'd tried to swim out of the way and was too tired to stay afloat and was now drowning on the other side of the well. She clawed her way over and lifted him up.

"Oh, Ro-*bair*! I'm so sorry!" He was coughing and spitting water in her face now. "Ro-*bair*! It's going to be alright, babe! You just hang on old Julia's arm and someone will find us!" He calmed down now, although he was still shivering and she realized, she was too; the water was mountain spring temperature, not like the eighty-degree day overhead.

How did she ever get in this position, she wondered? They don't even have wells like this in the States, they have to fill them in. But she'd always wanted to live in France. Right after her degree in French at Stanford she'd come over to stay in Paris for a few months on a Ravage fellowship. That was her family's joke. Their name was Ravage, and when she wanted to go places in the summer, taking summer courses, her dad would say, "Well, I guess we can manage another Ravage fellowship." The thing was, she was a serious student and everywhere she went she studied hard and learned what she was there for. The full-immersion French school. The computer school, where she'd learned how to type and produce desktop copy. And the postgrad semester in France was going to put her over the top in understanding French politics. The program almost promised a job as a journalist somewhere in France, following French affairs for some publication. And then she'd met Jean-Claude at the embassy party. She'd fallen head over heels in about two minutes flat, and her career was on hold. He'd been amazed that she wanted to make love the first night they were together. "Not like French women," he'd said. "They always want to get the rules established first." She didn't care about rules. She'd had a dizzying year following him around Europe on his assignments, going to all the parties, being his glamorous American companion, and on the vacations, wandering through the little villages in the Dordogne, lying on the beaches at St. Tropez, even the longer trips to Taormina, to Crete, and once, almost a dream, to the Seychelles, snorkeling in the unearthly blue lagoons, the *luxe* hotels, the endless sunsets with drinks and little bites of seafood hors d'oeuvres, the languorous lovemaking at night, or in the morning, or in the late afternoon before the nap, or after....

She'd never even hinted, only hoped and hoped, and then one rainy evening back in Paris he'd asked, "Julia, my love, can we go to Tours this weekend, to see Papa and Mama again?"

And she'd asked, "Why, we were just there a few weeks ago," and he said, "Because I want to tell them we are getting married."

Just like that. What she'd always dreamed of. Married to a rich, handsome French diplomat. A big flat in Paris, a vacation house near St. Raphael, right on the water, a condo at Courchevel—best skiing in Europe. And that was when she learned the difference between being a French mistress and a French wife. It was as if Jean-Claude had disappeared from her life. She realized suddenly that now she was expected to stay home while the diplomat went on his trips. "But you have your friends here, *cherie*," he said, surprised when she protested. "Marie, and Avril? And you always said you didn't see Helene enough? You are in Paris, my love! So many restaurants to try!" *Is that what I'm supposed to be now?* she wanted to know. *One of the ladies who lunch? And I hardly eat anything.* "And the clubs at night!" he went on. "The theater! You know Henri would die of ecstasy to take you around. He told me." She had to tell him that going around the clubs and the theatre with a darling gay actor was not her idea of a hot date.

Maybe he'll miss me and take me with him again, she hoped over and over. And then there was his picture on the cover of the tabloid. On a yacht off St. Tropez with other beautiful people, the women fashionably topless. The photo taken from shore with a telescopic lens by one of the hundreds of papparazzi who haunted the place. He had his arm around that singer, his hand just touching her nude breast.... She'd fled to Tours to see her mother-in-law, who'd been so kind to her, such a loving friend, nicer to her than her own mother, actually.

"My son is an idiot," his mother had said. "But this is what French husbands do, if they're rich and spoiled. He will just laugh it off and deny everything. And he feels no guilt at all, I can assure you."

So she showed everyone what American wives do. She divorced him. "I'm so sorry, darling," her mother-in-law had said. "In France the property settlement can take decades!" But she didn't care. And then she met Dan and everything was....

She lost her grip on the wood and went under again. This time she swallowed quite a bit of water and coughed harshly, Robert whimpering and trying to lick her face. How long had she been here? Had she been drifting off to sleep in the cold water, her mind wandering in the past, like explorers caught in a blizzard? She knew all about hypothermia, too, and knew that she could be so numbed by the cold that she'd just give up and slip under the water. She looked up at the well head. The sun was no longer hitting the edge; in fact it was much darker down here in the well now. She shuddered. Robert was now trembling uncontrollably. *Who's going to go first,* she wondered, *him or me?*

Dan came out of nowhere into her life. Her mother-in-law had dragged her to a party against her will, and there were all the most privileged people in France, chatting, drinking, eating, laughing— and smoking, of course. And she knew they were talking about her, a dumb American who couldn't forgive her husband a tiny affair, a meaningless thing. "Do you mind if I talk to you a bit?" he'd said. "I thought I could speak French, but everything's going too fast for me." And he gave her a wry smile. That was Dan. Julia thought her mother-in-law had arranged the meeting at first, but Madame was as surprised as everyone else. "An American author who thinks he can cook French food, if you can imagine. Michel brought him, my dear. Maybe he'll cook something for you." And he did, and it was delicious, and when they visited important restaurants and Dan went out to talk to the chef she could see that they respected his knowledge and asked him serious questions, nodded their heads when he explained his approach to certain dishes. *Eh voilà. Ça y'est. Vous comprenez!*

She heard French voices in the distance. Was someone coming? Once again she tried to call. Nothing. A croak no one would hear. "Ro-*bair*," she whispered. "Bark, bark, bark!" But he just nodded his head, looking at her wide-eyed, waiting for her to do something. The voices grew louder, and she realized they weren't French, it was

Timmy's in the Well

guttural, maybe Arabic, some farmworkers going home from the fields in the evening. From the sound they were abreast of the well now, and then the voices began to recede. Julia began to cry soundlessly and at that moment she thought of Dan, how she'd never see him again, how heartbroken he'd be, and she remembered one of the last times she'd seen him, standing there on the terrace, pursing his mouth and pretending to be the neighbor calling his dog, "Qui-*nou*...."

And then suddenly she was shaking Robert and croaking to him as loudly as she could, "Qui-*nou*! Qui-*nou*! Qui-*nou*!" And he yelped! "Yelp, yelp!"

"Yes! Yes!" she grunted hoarsely, "Qui-*nou*! Qui-*nou*! Qui*nou* is eating dinner, you little fucker, and here you are in the well!" And he yelped again, and then again and again and there was a noise above and dark faces looking in, and then there were shouts going up the path to the village and all she could murmur, sobbing, holding the piece of wood grimly now, was "Qui*nou*...Qui*nou*...Qui*nou*..."

The Olive Tree

Spencer was walking around in the garden, deep in thought, spooking the redstarts who were accustomed to rule the yard this time of day. Rosalind had been watching him, and when she reached a stopping point in the article she was typing on her computer she went out and joined him.

"What's on your mind, big guy?" She put an arm over his shoulder. They had made love the night before, and she was still feeling extra chummy.

"An olive tree," Spencer said, still concentrating on a spot on the ground in front of him. "An olive would be just right here in the corner. It would sort of balance the cherry over there. And the sun's just perfect. We could get a small one, and it would grow like a bastard in this soil and climate."

"It would be nice," Rosalind agreed. "But do we need an olive? How about an oleander? They flower half the year here."

"We could have olives. You know, olives from our own tree. Like we did back in Napa."

The Olive Tree

Rosalind thought about it, remembering picking the olives late every fall, slicing them with fingers turning purple, brining them, changing the brine every few days, finally serving them to guests, with Spencer bragging about *his* olives, from *his own* tree, although she usually did most of the work. And the guests politely tasting the obligatory one or two before turning gratefully to the smoked salmon. Sometimes she'd thrown out whole quart jars because they'd molded, Spencer could never figure out why.

"But the olives here are dirt cheap, Spence. Last time we were in St. Rémy? You know, at the market? The olive stalls had a thousand different kinds—we have some in the frigo right now."

But Spencer had convinced himself.

"We're in Provence, babe. We ought to have an olive!"

They had bought the old stone house four months ago. Spencer had figured out that he could handle his investments anywhere in the world on the net. Rosalind successfully wrote travel articles. After thinking about it a bit she had decided she could work anywhere too. Napa Valley had gotten smog-bound and awash with tourists all year long. And Provence was much closer to London, where she'd been born and grown up. She still had withdrawal symptoms.

After fifteen years with Spencer, Rosalind knew better than to argue. Besides, she thought, an olive tree would be nice. Maybe they ought to have a grape vine too, train it over an arbor to make some shade on the terrace. They could buy both plants at the same time. But their trip that afternoon to nurseries was frustrating. The grape vine was the easy part. But even in the garden sections of huge discount stores the little olive plants were absurdly expensive. Spencer was fuming.

"Three hundred fifty francs for a goddamned olive! That's more than fifty bucks. And did you see what a tiny thing they all were? Like a pencil! It'd take ten years before they'd bear!"

She agreed, tactfully, standing there with her grape vine on her hip in its five-liter plastic pot. They both remembered transplanting root stock from an old derelict olive grove back in northern California, just chopping volunteers loose from the growth around the base of an old tree and planting them in full sun overlooking the Napa Valley below their ranch. Olives were like weeds. In two years the trees had grown eight feet and started bearing fruit.

"You know," said Spencer, "I've seen neglected groves around here. I bet we could rescue some volunteers from there."

"I don't know," said Rosalind. "Maybe we should ask Jeannot."

So that evening they walked down to the café and put the problem to Jeannot. He was a former rugby player, huge and battered, a legendary star for France twenty years ago when they'd won the Five Nations championship. He owned the café and some local real estate. Spencer and Rosalind had bought their house through him and had found him marvelously friendly and helpful in dealing with all the complexities of French house-buying and furnishing. They sat in the bar facing his trophy wall with its montage of posters and photos of his greatest rugby triumphs, his desperation score against New Zealand in 1980, his impossible tackle of the Irish winger in 1986, all the photos surrounding his old jersey from his last game, the number three on it, still unwashed, with the copious blood stains drying black through the years.

"Ahah," he said, after hearing their story. "You don't like the price, so you want to steal from a neighbor. So soon you have become true Provençaux. Congratulations!"

Spencer started to protest, but Jeannot put up a huge hand. "No, no, my friend—I am joking. But you must realize, in France all land belongs to someone and to take something from someone's land is a serious crime. Ever since the Revolution, when they gave the peasants the land."

"But there's all sorts of neglected land around here," protested Rosalind. "All that church property outside the village. It's full of trees and fields."

"Yes, and not one olive," said Jeannot, smiling. "You see, when

The Olive Tree 97

the brothers went bankrupt, the next day you couldn't find a small plant anywhere on the property. It was all dug up and carried away during the night. The cherry trees are still there, of course, they're too big to carry away, but in cherry season the kids here in town pick them bare. No," he said, "you have to find a small tree on someone's property. But not a real olive grove. Only a tree someone is not taking care of. Otherwise you are in trouble. Last year old Arnaud took his neighbor to court because he picked one cherry, just walking past the orchard while Madame Arnaud was peeking out the window. And the Malécot woman was fined five hundred francs because she went in Pillod's vineyard in February, of all things, and picked up the leftover vine prunings. You should have seen her in the court, crying. 'But I just wanted to grill the sausages!' The magistrate didn't even look at her. 'Five hundred francs.' Bam! And everyone in the room knew Pillod was a sour old bastard, but they were thinking, 'What if it were my field?' Here in France you can cross anyone's field. But don't take anything!"

Spencer looked deflated, but Rosalind was beginning to look stubborn. Jeannot recognized the attitudes.

"All right, my friends. I'll tell you. Walk around the neighborhood, then tell me what you find. Maybe there are some deserted properties no one is taking care of." And he winked.

The next day Spencer set out for a long walk, having borrowed Rosalind's bird-watching binoculars as cover. He had already thought of a target. On the hill behind town there was an old derelict *mas*, a country house surrounded by a two-meter-high stone wall. The owners were rich old people in Paris who never came here. He and Rosalind had often walked by on the path that led up the hill, then through Fouquet's cherry orchard, then down a country road to the main road back home. Once they had stopped to peek through the locked and chained gate across the driveway. They saw nothing but overgrown brush, trees, vines, going every which way.

As they turned away they had been confronted by a little old man who had emerged from a tiny cottage across the road.

"That is private property," he had shouted in heavily accented Provençal French. "I am the caretaker. I can call the police at any time!" It was old Raymond, Jeannot told Spencer. A mean old man, as nosy as an old woman.

This time Spencer kept to the back side of the property, concealed by the heavy underbrush along the path. He remembered a spot where a low oak tree limb overhung the wall, and he thought he'd take a look into the property, see if he could spot any old olive trees. Rosalind had warned him about the wall.

"They put broken glass in the mortar on top of the wall when they're building it, you know. Mind you don't try to jump up with your hands on the wall." She told Spencer the old estates in England had broken glass on the walls too.

"My God! What if someone cut their hands…the insurance.…" Spencer had been about to say, when he realized what a typically absurd American reaction that was.

When he reached the oak he was looking for, he did, nevertheless, feel the top of the wall gingerly. Yes, his fingers told him, there was broken glass on top of the wall. So it was up the tree, then.

He had been thinking of his youth, when he had scampered up tree trunks, branch to branch, to look into the next yard, where the neighbors' teenage daughter from time to time lay in the sun with her top off to get an all-over tan. Without that sort of incentive, and now suddenly conscious of twenty extra pounds and what he thought of as a firm and muscular stomach that still seemed to get in the way of narrow spaces between tree limbs, Spencer attained the branch he was looking for, panting, sweating, and with a painful bruise on his thigh from a sharp stub of a branch. He inched out along the limb until he was over the wall. To the left he could see nothing but rank underbrush. He turned to the right. There, in full view, was a small, miserably neglected stand of olive trees. The smallest had the diameter of a broomstick and was five feet high. Spencer was thinking that a little tree like that, watered and fertilized in a friendly yard, would grow at least six feet in a year and soon be ready to produce fruit.

He fixated on the tree, imagining the scraggly limbs becoming stout, reaching into the heavens, putting out tiny bunches of flowers to become tiny green fruits no larger than peas in the summer, then swelling in the autumn, growing, growing, plump and green until the magic days of late December, when they started turning black and could be picked, sliced, brined, turned into impressive appetizers....

He became conscious of a rhythmic noise beneath him. He looked down and perceived a large rottweiler sitting just below him and looking up with joyous expectation, tongue lolling out, panting, but with no intention of barking, as a stupid shepherd would have done, just waiting for the moment when the intruder might drop down into his territory and provide the moment he had been trained for all his life.

"Bon chiot!" said Spencer in the friendliest tone he could muster. *Good puppy!* The rottweiler cocked an ear, heard the unfamiliar accent, and just barely lifted a lip in a silent snarl. He shifted his hind feet as if seeking a firmer stance from which to leap up the wall.

"These damned French with their damned German dogs!" raged Spencer to Rosalind when he got home. "Haven't they ever heard of a golden retriever, a Lab, some nice dog like that?"

"It's the burglars, darling," said Rosalind, trying to calm him down. "We ourselves have twenty thousand francs' worth of burglar prevention with an alarm connection to the police. Most local people can't afford that. So they have German dogs. It's a lot cheaper. And the dogs will wake up when a thief comes in the night, not like the lout our village calls a policeman."

"Wake up! That's it, my sweet! Wake up! You're a genius!" Spencer was on his feet, dancing with joy. "We just have to make sure the dog doesn't wake up. Your pills! You must have something…" and he went into the bathroom, where Rosalind could hear him rooting through drawers. He emerged with a bottle of valium in one hand and several capsules of Dormitol, a French prescription sleeping pill, in the other.

"Remember your back pain? And the doctor in Apt said you'd sleep like a baby? How many of these do you think…"

"Well, remember, a rottweiler doesn't weigh what a human—"

"Oh come on! That bastard is sixty kilos if he's an ounce. He'll outweigh you ten pounds at least!"

"Maybe a couple…and some Valium to relax him…" Rosalind was getting into the pharmaceutical spirit of things. "And you remember," she added. "Andy left that pipe half-full of hashish last May?"

"Do I remember? It was monstrous! I could barely walk after one puff. And I've been tempted to throw it away. But do you think a dog would eat hashish?"

"Christ, Spencer! Have you ever seen a big dog eat? He'll have half a can of dog food full of pills and hash down his throat in two seconds!" She giggled. "I wish I could see it."

"You mean you're not coming with me?"

"Sorry, Spence. I don't do olive trees."

"Well then. But you'll have to go get the dog food. All right?"

"Fine. I can do dog food."

But Rosalind began to wonder the next day at the village grocer's. She had intended to go to the supermarket in Apt, where she could buy dog food anonymously, but she'd been too busy and finally just walked down the block to Henri's little *épicerie* in the village. As usual Henri was talking, laughing, joking, gossiping with everyone in the store as he checked them out, and her heart fell when he finally got around to her purchases. Out of the pile of coffee, rice, cereal, mineral water, and onions he immediately snatched the can

The Olive Tree   101

of dog food and gestured with it to the whole store, babbling away in French.

"Ah, Madame! You are buying a dog! A wise move. The thieves are everywhere these days!"

"No, no," interrupted Rosalind hastily, in her adequate French. "I'm just picking up a can for a friend."

"You have a friend with a dog, then?" Rosalind was about to make up some other lie, but to her relief Henri, as usual, couldn't resist joking.

"Or maybe he's going to eat the dog food himself? Ha ha! Better than the paté you get at some stores. But you know, a woman came in, oh, last spring, and said she actually wanted dog food for her husband."

The crowd in the store grew silent. They knew that Henri was going to tell one of his famous stories.

"She'd read that this certain dog food would improve her husband's…you know what I mean!" And Henri grinned and winked shamelessly. There was a ripple of mirth in the crowd. Most of them had heard the story.

"So the next week she came back and bought two cases of the same dog food. I thought, *That man must be like a stallion by now!* But I didn't ask. How could I?

"Well, two weeks later she came in and you could see she'd been crying. So I ask, 'How is your husband with the dog food—does it make him…you know?'

"But she just starts crying again, blubbering away, and finally says, 'He's…he's dead.'"

Henri did a good impression of a woman blubbering. "So I said, 'I knew that much dog food couldn't be healthy!' And she says 'No, no. It wasn't the food. Yesterday he was lying in the street licking his balls and a bus ran over him.'"

Rosalind escaped with her purchases amid the general laughter, hoping that no one would remember she'd bought dog food.

Spencer had been at his computer, trading on the internet all morning. Along with his blue chips he had begun experimenting with selling flashy cybertech stocks short. A week ago he'd taken a big gamble. Today he redeemed the stock he had shorted at a third of its cost and came out over $14,000 ahead once he'd paid the commissions and the interest on his margin account. So he was in a good mood when Rosalind came home.

He laughed uproariously at the dog food story. "Hey! That's a funny joke! I wonder where an imbecile like Henri heard it?"

"Probably in the French edition of *Playboy*," said Rosalind. "But the joke's surely as old as the Hittites."

"Did the Hittites have dog food?" asked Spencer and roared again at his own wit.

"I don't know, but you can explain, next time Henri runs into you and asks you how the stuff is working." Rosalind was grumpy, but cheered up at the news of the stock market coup, and they were soon in the kitchen, mixing dog food with Valium, Dormitol, and hashish, arguing over the ratio of ingredients.

"Maybe we shouldn't use the hash," said Rosalind. "If you got caught…you know how the French are about drugs."

"I think the French are even tougher about poisoning someone's dog," said Spencer. "Anyway, no one's going to catch me. I'm going to go out at one o'clock this morning. The moon's going to be almost full. You know this town. On a weeknight there's no one awake at eleven, let alone at one."

"If you say so," said Rosalind. "But dress warmly. It's still cold these nights."

Spencer stayed up and watched a movie on television. It was an American gangster movie dubbed into French, and he understood only a bit of the dialogue, but the movie was action driven and the plot was senseless anyway.

Inspired by the violence and fortified with several little glasses of Armagnac, he set out silently a little after one A.M., wearing his good pigsuede jacket and a backpack containing a short spade and a sturdy hatchet normally used for firewood. In a plastic bag was the enchanted gobbet of dog food.

The outer lanes of the village were completely deserted, and a slight mist obscured the street lights. Spencer soon left the lights behind on the path up the hill and was gratified to see the forest ahead of him illuminated by the brilliance of the full moon. He soon reached the designated oak tree and began to climb carefully, making just enough noise to alert a guard dog. This time he managed to evade the sadistic sharp limb that had wounded his thigh the last time. He found the long branch that reached out over the wall and was wondering whether the rottweiler was on the job or not when a piercing bark from below nearly made him lose his grip. He peered frantically down into the gloom. There was the rottweiler indeed, no longer mute but threatening to bark again.

"Bon chiot!" said Spencer in his most reassuring tone, struggling to extract the dog bait from the top of his pack. Luckily the big dog fell silent, looking upward now in anticipation. Spencer extracted the wad of dog food, making a filthy mess of his right hand, and held it out. *"Bon appetit!"* he said, and let the ball fall to the ground.

The rottweiler was on it in a second, but suddenly paused and looked up into the tree. Spencer was beginning to worry that this was a trained guard dog and would refuse any food except from its master. But he had nothing to fear. After the one suspicious glance the big dog took a single whiff of the morsel at its feet, wolfed it down in two swift gulps, and looked up eagerly for more. Now all Spencer had to do was wait.

He had actually not thought about the length of time it would take to suitably drug a large dog. The branch he was lying on got harder and rougher on his chest and stomach, and the chill of the night began to penetrate even through his leather jacket and woolen sweater. Beneath him the dog continued to mount a vigil, now and then wandering off to the right or left as if to make sure that no other path of invasion had been left open. The creature did not bark again, fortunately.

It was close to three o'clock when Spencer finally saw the big head begin to lower, then jerk suddenly erect again, a reaction familiar to Spencer himself from his days in college lecture halls. Then the dog started wandering again, this time aimlessly. He looked confused and once tried to bark but it only came out as a muffled "woof," and finally he headed back toward the front of the estate, staggering once and with difficulty regaining his feet.

All was going as planned, Spencer thought. But he waited for another frozen ten minutes before wriggling to the end of the branch. First he took off the pack and dropped it to the ground. Then he laboriously turned himself around so he could lower himself enough to drop to the ground himself, which he did clumsily, falling noisily into the underbrush. He held his breath for a moment, terrified that the dog would reappear.

But silence reigned, and Spencer slowly got to his feet and tiptoed with the pack over to the olive orchard. As if an omen, the moon came out from behind a patch of mist and shone directly on the little tree he'd seen the other day. The silvery leaves gleamed in the moonlight. Spencer set to work as quietly as he could, shoveling dirt away from the base of the tree until the clump of roots stopped his spade. From experience he knew that he could cut the outlying roots with a hatchet and then bend the tree this way and that until the roots at the bottom either broke or could be cut as well. The tree would recover quickly and grow new roots once it was back in the ground again.

He'd forgotten how time-consuming it was to uproot an olive, particularly if one wished to preserve a fairly large root ball, so the sight of the moon dropping below the trees to the west just as the olive finally came free from the ground alarmed Spencer. He consulted his watch and saw that he'd been working for a half-hour. He had no idea how long the dog would be suitably drugged. He

The Olive Tree   105

therefore set to work quickly, filling the hole in the earth, smoothing the ground around it, and strewing leaves and brush at random until the site looked like the surrounding wilderness. Then he put spade and hatchet in his pack and lobbed it over the wall. There was a satisfying *clunk* on the other side. He now began to swing the tree with its heavy ball of roots and earth, planning to swing it to the top of the wall where he could lever it over.

But on the back swing Spencer suddenly heard the thunder of great paws behind him. In his apprehensive mood it sounded every bit like Ben Hur coming in his chariot. He frantically jumped sideways in time to see the huge dark shape of the rottweiler surge past him and run directly head first into the wall. He was preparing to hurl himself up the wall, olive tree forgotten, when he saw that the dog was lying motionless. *My God! Did I kill the poor thing?* he thought, and rapidly began swinging the tree again. A-one, a-two, and a-three. He gave it a tremendous swing and the tree actually cleared the wall. He could hear it crash down on the other side.

Spencer now considered his last obstacle, to climb back across the wall. He had planned to leap up, seize the overhanging limb and use it to get a foot on top of the wall, avoiding the broken glass. His first two attempts failed as his shoe skidded off the edge of the wall. Then he had to release the limb and take a few deep breaths to get his wind back. Finally he determined to put everything into the effort. *What am I?* he thought, *some puny wimp? I used to be an athlete!* And he leaped up to grab the tree limb, swinging his left shoe up onto the wall. His heel dug in satisfactorily, and now he started to twist, hugging the tree limb and trying to bring up his right leg. But his right leg wasn't coming up, caught on something, he thought, shaking it. Spencer was about to jump back down and he gave a quick glance to see what was preventing his leg from coming up. He cried out in dismay at the terrible sight.

There was the rottweiler, at least partially revived, jaws locked around his running shoe. The dog was still obviously groggy and was sort of staggering around, but the strength of its jaws was there...and increasing. As Spencer desperately tried to shake his foot free, the dog began to growl.

"Oh, my God!" whimpered Spencer, and in a great spasm he jerked up on his right foot as hard as he could. His foot slipped right out of his shoe, and suddenly he was free. But the momentum threw him onto the wall and he convulsed in pain as his left leg ground against the spikes of broken glass.

"Aarghh!" Spencer shrilled through clenched teeth. With a herculean effort he pulled himself back onto the oak limb. But his chest brushed against the top of the wall and he felt a puncture of sharp glass in his chest before he was able to rip his jacket free. Finally he could slither back down the tree on the other side of the wall to retrieve his treasure. The tree did not neglect to rip at his groin with the sharp broken stub on the way down.

Then all Spencer could do was look with horror at his olive tree. It was lying directly across the prostrate figure of a little old man whose face was obscured by Spencer's pack. It seemed obvious. Old Raymond had somehow heard or suspected him and had crept up on the outside of the wall, planning...what? To confront him with his theft? No, worse. There was a shotgun lying in the brush. So the old man had been going to trap him, maybe shoot him. And then Spencer had thrown the pack containing the hatchet and shovel over the wall and hit Raymond right on the head, knocking him unconscious. Then the dog had attacked. Then Spencer had thrown the tree over to land directly on the man's abdomen. Could he be alive?

Spencer gingerly felt a grimy wrist for a pulse, then almost collapsed in relief. There was a strong pulse, and now he could hear labored breathing and smell the reek of poorly digested food and too much wine. Steeling his nerves, calming himself, Spencer now gathered up his pack and his tree. He could do nothing about his lost shoe, so he began to creep carefully down the path towards town, hobbling on his one bare foot. As he was reaching the outskirts of

The Olive Tree 107

the village he heard a dog on the hill behind him begin to bay in pain and despair, starting up a chorus of every other dog in town. But his back gate was near, and he slipped quickly through it.

The clock in the seventeenth century church was striking four o'clock in the morning when Rosalind finally finished bandaging Spencer's cuts from the broken glass. There were two small ones on his chest where the sharp points had gone right through his leather jacket. But there were three serious slashes on his left calf from when he'd heaved himself up onto the branch. He'd barely felt the cuts at the time, but now they were smarting miserably in spite of liberal annointing with Erythrogel, a powerful prescription antibiotic.

"At least it won't get infected," said Rosalind. "But I really think you need some stitches." She'd shaved his leg all around the cuts, medicated them, and bandaged them tightly.

"God! They really hurt. Give me another glass of the Armagnac, babe."

"Spence, I don't know—the ointment package says alcohol is *déconseillé*—it might cause an adverse reaction. You know, we could go to Dr. Beauvais tomorrow. He could put in a few stitches and maybe prescribe a painkiller—"

"Sure! And two minutes later everyone in town knows that I have glass cuts on my leg. And there's probably blood all over the top of the wall! Oh, Christ, it stings so!" Spencer was being a baby, a condition Rosalind never discouraged.

"Oh, poor Spence! You'll have to tough it out then. At least we have some Valium and Dormitol left."

"Thank God! Give me a few."

"Actually, they're mixed in with the dog food we didn't use. And there's the hashish in there too. That could be a plus. You know, they say the dog food's not bad at all. We could warm it up with a little oil and garlic...."

ʃ

A few days later Spencer strolled down the main street of town through the towering plane trees to Jeannot's café, disguising the pain of walking on his torn leg with a studied lassitude, as if suddenly fully aware of the enchanting Provençal village.

Taking a table outside under the trees and talking to Jeannot, he could see into the bar, where a ray of sun lightened Jeannot's trophy wall and the bloody jersey. It only reminded Spencer of his own wounds.

"So, you took the olive tree!" said Jeannot. "What luck! Now you are one of us!"

Spencer had told the whole story, knowing that Jeannot, alone of all the villagers, would never disclose a confidence, at least not while it remained a sensitive issue.

"Yes, but I'm worried sick. I know the police were up there at the *mas*, looking at the wall and everything else. And they've got my other shoe!" Spencer was whispering intently.

"The shoe? I don't know…fingerprints? Who knows? If you have never been fingerprinted in France there is no comparison, *hein*? And I talked to the police, being very concerned, of course. They told me they could find no crime, nothing stolen, only the blood on the wall, and they think old Raymond was just drunk and imagining things. The shoe? They said the dog probably found it somewhere and brought it home. What did you do with the hole from the olive tree?"

"I filled it in with dirt and scattered leaves around it."

"*Voilà!* No one knows there is an olive tree missing. So, my friend, I think you have a free olive tree, aside from the cost of your coat and your pants. How much did you pay for the leather coat, did you say?"

Spencer started grumbling about the ruined clothes, but Jeannot's attention was distracted by the view down the street, seeing Raymond himself trudging toward them. The old man had a bandage tied around his head, and he was holding a huge rottweiler

The Olive Tree   109

on a long leash, letting the dog circulate among the tables outside
the two other cafés along the tree-lined lane. Most arresting was the
sight of the large running shoe in Raymond's other hand, which he
frequently held out for the dog to sniff.

Should I say something? Jeannot thought. *Or maybe just let things
take their course. It is the Provençal way, after all. And who knows what
will happen?*

Story Time

When the girl heard Missy coming she quickly hid her writing pad and pretended to be watching television. Missy came in with a big smile on her face, went over to close the blinds against the afternoon sun fading the rug.

"We've got a surprise for you today, Amy." She came over to Amy's wheelchair, took a hairbrush off the dresser, and began to brush the girl's long brown hair gently. Missy nodded at the television.

"You'll like your surprise better than 'Miss Brooks' I bet," she said.

Amy couldn't figure out what Missy was talking about for a moment. Then she realized the show she was pretending to watch was something about Miss Brooks.

"I'm through watching," she said. "You can turn it off if you want."

Missy turned off the television, then came back to tuck Amy's

Story Time

blanket around her. Her hand encountered the writing pad under the blanket, and she pulled it out.

"Oh, have you been keeping your diary again, Amy? Can I peek at it sometime?" she asked archly, one eyebrow raised.

"Maybe someday," said Amy, seriously. "But I'd rather you didn't right now. Okay?"

Missy smiled primly. "I'm sorry, honey. I didn't mean to pry." She tucked the writing pad back down under the blanket again.

She wheeled Amy down the hall and into the library, sunny and light with the sun streaming in.

"And there's your surprise!"

Amy saw a gleaming cream-colored computer on a new desk with a keyboard mounted just below and a printer to the side. Her mouth fell open, but she couldn't say a word.

"Doctor Bob thought you might like it. Your teacher from last year said you were the best at the computer in the whole sixth grade."

Missy wheeled Amy over and carefully pushed her in until her knees were under the keyboard. Amy immediately picked up the mouse, pulled down the menu to the left of the screen, and studied it intently.

"Has it got Story yet?"

"Story? You mean a word-processing program?"

"Uh huh. I had Story last year. It was fun, and I wrote some stories. I'm a good typist."

"Well, Doctor Bob said he had some things to add. He needs to use it sometimes himself. Maybe he'll put it in later today." Missy did her best to sound as if she knew computers and all their habits.

"In the meantime, Doctor Bob left you a bunch of games." She held out a handful of CDs. Amy took them, shuffled through them rapidly. "The Princess and the Goblins," "Treasure Island," "Animal Farm...." *A bunch of junk*, she thought. But she smiled.

"These look neat. I'll have to try them." She did her best to sound enthusiastic.

As soon as Missy had left, Amy pulled out her writing pad. She'd filled almost four pages, single-spaced, since yesterday and her fingers were beginning to cramp. She propped the pad up behind the keyboard and started trying to find the built-in Simple Text that came with the computer. It wasn't a very good writing program, but at least she could type her story so far, and then when Doctor Bob put in Story, she could transfer it and make it a Story file.

Amy looked over the first page of her writing pad. It was messy. She'd corrected some spellings and crossed out things here and there. Now she could make a neat copy. She liked to start stories by taking a situation from some TV commercial. Commercials showed you interesting people, people you'd like to meet, but the minute you got involved they would drink beer or drive off in a pickup or something. Amy figured she could give them more exciting lives than that.

She began to copy her text.

Hank pulled his dusty red pickup off the highway and into the restaurant parking lot. He got out, wiping his forehead. The sun was almost overhead and hot in the sky. He clomped towards the little café in his well-worn boots. An old brown dog lying in the shade of the gas pumps looked up at him and wagged his tail lazily.

Janey saw him come through the door first. She was behind the counter, hot and sweating, just waiting for lunch to end so she could go somewhere else boring. She saw a tall, slim young guy just standing there looking around, pushing his hat back, the old guys in the room checking out the newcomer, them in their overalls and tractor caps. Then he saw Janey and he gave her a big smile that lit up the whole room. The old guys went back to their coffee and chili, and it was like there was just the two of them there.

Hank came over to the counter and sat down on a stool,

Story Time   113

sighing. He propped his tan arms on the counter and cocked his head at Janey.

"I got tired of all this fast food stuff, last couple of days, you know? It's about all you can find on the highway anymore."

"It won't be fast, but it'll be food, anyways, here," said Janey, laughing. She had a teasing way about her.

"You mean good old home-cooked American food?"

"It's like home-cooked, but in this place it's Indian," said Janey with an arch grin.

"Indian? You mean curry and like that?"

"Never heard of the Curry Indians," she said. "Round here you're going to get Blackfoot...Ray!" she called over her shoulder.

A face appeared at the window to the kitchen, high cheek-bones, flat. Black eyes expressionless. The cook had a long black braid hanging down his back.

Amy heard a door open, and Doctor Bob came in saying something over his shoulder to Missy. He turned to Amy.

"Hi there, scamp! What are you up to today?"

Amy quickly put her file away. "I'm just writing some stuff, Bob. Thank you so much for the computer. I just love it!"

Doctor Bob looked embarrassed.

"You don't have to thank me, honey," he said. "That's all provided for by...." He stopped for a second. "All provided for, and just about anything else you want."

Provided for by the insurance, Amy thought. She was going to change the subject, but Doctor Bob spoke first.

"Missy said you asked for a Story program. I had this disk at home and I thought I'd just bring it by and we'll put it in your machine. You're supposed to buy a new one every time but we won't tell, okay?"

Amy laughed. "I won't. Anyway, sometimes the older programs are better...simpler, at least."

They put the disk in and followed all the installation instructions. The computer was strong and fast and almost immediately it told them *Installation successful.*

"There we go!" said Doctor Bob. "Now, what are you going to write? And can I read it?"

Amy squirmed. "Well...I don't...."

Doctor Bob saw her discomfort and cut in, "Now, don't you worry, Amy. You write anything you want. If you want to show us, that's fine. If you want it to be private, we'll never, ever pressure you. I know some of the greatest writers *never* showed their work to anyone until it was done."

And sometimes even after it was done, thought Amy. But she just smiled and started asking the doctor other questions. He helped her transfer her document to Story and made a point of looking away rapidly when her story came up on the screen for a moment.

"There you are, honey. You know this program, don't you?"

"Oh, yes! We learned it at school last year. In fact, I had to show Daddy how to use it for his reports."

Doctor Bob smiled, patted her on the shoulder, and walked out of the library into the hallway. Missy had been waiting there for him.

"I heard what she said...about her Daddy. I want to cry every time she—" The doctor shushed her and they walked down the hall for a bit.

"I know, I know what you mean," he said. "But it's good that she can talk about them. And the writing is excellent therapy."

"You don't think she's writing about...."

"No, it's just a story. I saw 'Blackfoot' in there."

"A black foot? What in the world...?"

"No, no. 'Blackfoot' as in Blackfoot Indians." The doctor saw from her expression that she still didn't get it. He sighed and went on alone into his office. Convalescent home nurses were not always intellectual giants. But at least Missy was sweet and kind.

Story Time   115

⁊

"Hey, Ray, what's best today, the chicken fried steak or the chili size?" Janey turned to Hank again. "It's one or the other. Everything else here is lousy." She made a face and giggled.

Hank looked her over carefully. He saw a happy face, a wicked grin, mischief in the eyes. She was average cute, but he was attracted by her kidding. He liked women who were happy and kidded around. There were too few of them these days, he thought. Janey was wearing an extra-large T-shirt and short shorts under her apron. She started tapping her fingers on the counter.

"Okay. I think I'll have the steak. I get biscuits with that?"

"Unless we ran out. I'll see. And cream gravy too."

One of the men at a side table called to her. "Hey, Janey! I get some more coffee here? Or you gonna spend all day with your beau?"

Janey called into the kitchen. "It's the steak, Ray. Biscuits with the gravy, if we got any left." Then she drew a cup from the coffee machine and walked from behind the counter to take the man his coffee. Hank checked out her figure. She had a nice behind and long, tan legs. She looked back suddenly, caught him checking her out, and wiggled a hip at him, smirking.

Amy stopped writing for a moment. She was remembering how her father would watch her mother walking across the room. And her mother would whirl around and say, "Caught you, you dirty old man! What are you thinking about? What would your wife say?" And then maybe she'd wiggle her behind and they'd both laugh. Then sometimes if they both started laughing and kidding around after a while they'd go upstairs. Amy was wondering if she would have Hank and Janey doing something like that. It seemed like so much fun, but once when she'd written a story at school about a girl and a really neat guy her teacher had this worried look on her face, and she must have told her mom because her mom told her to write all the stories that came into her head but to keep them secret.

"For school, just make up stories about things we've seen, you know, everyday things," she'd said. "And you can add makeup things to make the stories more interesting. You know, like the other day at the market when that lady got mad at the woman with the food stamps."

So Amy had written a story about a nasty lady who got mad at poor people using food stamps, but when the lady started checking her own things out the manager caught her shoplifting a bottle of vodka. It was funny, but her teacher didn't like that story either.

"What would your wife say, she saw you looking at other girls like that?" said Janey, laughing, coming back behind the counter.

"She'd say I still had a dirty mind," said Hank, grinning. "But I don't have a wife anymore. Did, but she picked up and went."

Janey's face fell. "Oh, I'm sorry. I didn't mean to...."

"No problem." Hank sort of looked down into his cup of coffee. "Guess it was just one of those things, you know, college sweethearts."

"Yeah. I know all about your college sweethearts deal," said Janey, and for once her smile sort of twisted into a scowl. "I did a couple years at Boise State and had to get away from there because...." She shook her head, smiled again. "Enough of that stuff. Tell me, what're you doin' on the road, old pickup like that?"

"Movin' on, movin' on," said Hank. "Left all that hurt behind. Got a pretty good chance at a job in Seattle. Turns out I do the kind of computer programming they're looking for, so they said come on out and let's see what you can do." He looked up directly into her eyes.

Story Time   117

"I'll be there tomorrow. Want to come with me?"

Janey met his eyes, started taking her apron off and called into the kitchen. "Ray? I'm outta here." She turned back to Hank, her face alight. "Let's get going, Mr. Computer Dude. Seattle's fine with me."

Hank was getting up, his face suddenly unsure.

"Won't your boss get mad?"

Janey laughed, turned to the kitchen. "Hey, Ray? You mad at me?"

The impassive face appeared at the kitchen window. He looked at Janey, over at Hank, then back.

"No. Hell no. Good luck." Then he disappeared.

"I mean, your boss, the owner here...." Hank began to stutter.

"Ray is the owner, big guy." Janey grabbed him by the arm, steering him toward the door. "What's the problem? You getting cold feet?"

Hank took her by both arms, looked seriously into her face. He realized he didn't even know her name.

"No, no cold feet. You and me, babe, forever. I'd kiss you, but I don't even know your name."

One of the old ranchers spoke up, "It's Janey, you dumb jerk, and if you two kids don't get outta this lousy town quick, you'll be stuck here forever." The whole room burst into laughter.

"I'm Hank," said Hank. "Don't you want to get any clothes?"

"I hate all my clothes," said Janey. She reached up and kissed him, and they walked out to the truck.

Mrs. Largo was concerned. She was the director of the convalescent home and had to answer to a board of directors, so that's what her normal look was, concerned. But now she was extra concerned. She had Doctor Bob with her, looking at Amy's story.

"I really don't think Amy should be getting involved with stories about…about, you know…well, it's obvious what's going on in this story!"

Doctor Bob owed his appointment to Mrs. Largo, so he had to look serious too. But he tried to calm her down.

"Well, I can see what you mean. But I think it's really harmless. I mean, it's just romance, and a girl her age is going to think about romance." He chuckled.

"But that's just it," said Mrs. Largo. She was a thin woman with a thin face, who wore very pale lipstick on her thin lips and had big hair a disconcerting shade of caramel.

"Can't you see? The poor girl isn't going to be able to have any kind of…you know, romance, with her injuries. Why encourage her to fantasize? Don't you agree?"

Doctor Bob obviously didn't agree. In fact, he looked very angry. But he forced himself to adopt the expression of a true scientist, considering every contingency.

"Well, you could be right, Dorothy. But she's a sweet little girl. Who can tell what's going to happen in her—"

Mrs. Largo was not used to other contingencies than the ones she herself had selected. "I want you to monitor her writing very carefully," she said. "If this obsession goes on.…" And she considered the subject closed and left the room. Doctor Bob carefully restored Amy's story to the file name on the screen, "Janey and Hank," and then paused, as if thinking very carefully about something. Then he left too.

Janey and Hank were driving down the long country road in the dusty red pickup. It was getting dark, and the surrounding mountains were shading from tan down into dark purple. They hadn't stopped talking since they'd left the restaurant.

"Hey, wait a minute," said Hank. "We keep telling each other our life stories, we won't have anything else to say and we'll be like boring old married people."

Story Time 119

"You doofus!" said Janey, punching him on the arm. "Didn't you know old married people can know everything about each other and be even more in love?"

Hank looked over at her for a long moment. "Only one way to find out," he grinned. "How about getting married?"

Ahead of them a few miles on the winding road, coming their direction, was a big lumber truck. It started climbing a long grade and began to slow down. Behind it was a smaller truck. Its driver was annoyed and looked ahead down the road. Looked all clear, so he pulled out to pass. The lumber truck driver didn't feel like getting passed by another truck, so he accelerated as much as he could on the hill. The two trucks mounted the slope straining, side by side, up towards the crest, neither one giving an inch.

At that moment, Janey spotted a sign ahead: THE TIMBERS MOTEL.

"It's like the Bible says," said Janey. "And a sign appeared to Abraham. You know, there's nothing else ahead until Shelby, 'bout an hour or so."

"My name's not Abraham," said Hank. "But a sign is a sign." And he pulled into the Timbers.

Mrs. Largo was looking at the computer screen, her tiny lips pressed angrily together. She hesitated, as if about to go call Doctor Bob again. Then she smiled to herself grimly, sat down at the keyboard and changed the last few lines to

"Then we'd better get on to Shelby and find a minister," said Hank."

Then she left for home.

Amy screamed in her sleep and woke up. Once again she could see the hill ahead of them on the country road, and then suddenly the two trucks coming over the crest and roaring down on them....

"No, no!" she shrieked, and threw herself out of bed, her poor legs flopping on the floor. Hand over hand she clawed her way over the rug to her wheelchair and desperately pulled herself up into its seat, then frantically wheeled her way through the doorway and down the darkened hallway to the library.

Her computer was asleep, so she pounded a few keys. "Please, please!" she whispered, willing the screen to light up again. And there was the terrible sentence!

Amy's fingers had never flown so fast. Boom! She deleted the horrible invader's words. *Tap, tappity tappity tappity tap!* She restored the last sentence.

"My name's not Abraham," said Hank. "But a sign is a sign."
And he turned into the Timbers.

Amy punched the window key and a box came up saying "Do you want to save the changes you made to Janey and Hank"?

"Yes, yes, yes!" she moaned and clicked the save button. The screen went blank and she sank back into her wheelchair, tears of relief pouring down her cheeks. "Oh, yes, yes, thank you, thank you!"

Mrs. Largo was on her way home down a country road. Ahead of her a dusty red pickup turned into a motel and for a moment it reminded her of something. But it must not have been important so she put it out of her mind, driving up toward the crest of the next hill, self-righteous to the last.

Starting All Over Again

The doctor got there right away when he called. Then the doctor called the funeral home, and they came, got ready to take her away. The doctor—Vines, that was his name—asked if he had relatives, children, whatever, where he could stay for the rest of the night. No, he said, he wouldn't wake them up this time of night. Then the doc asked if he wanted a tranquillizer. Dr. Vines was very concerned about his state of mind. No, he said. I knew it was coming. I can get along tonight, the rest of tonight, what's left. Doctor Vines left in his car, the funeral home van left, the sheriff's car left; he had no idea why the sheriff had come. Maybe just proving they were always on hand, justify their budget.

He sat in his comfortable leather chair, there in the living room, for maybe an hour, trying to figure out what he thought about his loss, losing Florence, finally putting a name to her. Florence. She was gone now.

A light was beginning to fill the room, coming from over the hill to the east. He'd lost track of time, but it was the sun coming up, it was almost six in the morning and the sun was rising. The yellow light illuminated the living room through the blinds, coming from the high windows facing the east. He could make out the big desk in the corner, the paintings on the wall. The bookshelves, all around the room, jammed with the collections of forty years.

As the light hit the first rose in the garden he rose, slowly, putting his hands on his hips and creaking his back, getting ready to move. Out through the back door he trudged in his slippers and picked up the hose. Turned it on, gently. He walked through the garden, watering Florence's roses. They wouldn't last a day, she'd said, not in this climate, unless you water them, lay down a pool around the roots. Don't ever spray on the leaves, you'll make mildew. He could smell the pretty smelling ones, not even being near them. They all had names, but he didn't know them. Roses was roses. The sun from the east was beginning to pick them out, and as the rays hit each bud the perfume got stronger. And then suddenly he felt hungry. He'd filled the little basins under the roses fairly well so he went in, trying to think what he'd have for breakfast.

In the kitchen he turned on one burner, reached below for a nonstick pan. He'd butter a piece of bread, put it in the pan for a few minutes, and have a piece of fried bread, always tastier than just plain toast from the toaster. Butter. He could put on as much as he liked now and he grinned a little at the thought.

Reaching to his left toward the silverware drawer, his hand encountered the begonia in the pot that Florence had established on the kitchen counter. He usually did a lot of the cooking, but Florence had rules about where things went, and she liked the begonia pot right there, to the left of the stove. It seemed like anything he wanted to do he was sticking his hand in the begonia.

He picked up the begonia pot, moved to the kitchen door, and threw the begonia pot out into the yard. After all, he thought, Florence doesn't care where her begonia is now. As he closed the door

Starting All Over Again 123

he heard a familiar sound at his feet. Little Jasper was there, meowing, looking up at him imploringly. The little cat never got to go out. Their last cat, Climber, had been an outdoor cat but had disappeared. Everyone in the neighborhood knew what had happened. When the drought started the coyotes had begun to move into town, moving up the little stream bed that ran through their neighborhood. Some coyote had eaten Climber. They'd called her Climber because she was such a sweet, clinging cat, would climb up your leg if you didn't pay attention and go to sleep on your lap.

He reached down and patted Jasper, then put out some canned cat food for him. But Jasper had seen the door open and he ignored his food, went over to the door and meowed again. Poor cat, he'd never been out but he never gave up hope, looking out there in the garden, seeing the birds pecking around on the ground.

"Okay, Jasper," he said. "You're an outdoor cat from now on." And he opened the door and let him out. He figured he could get one of those cat doors, put it in the kitchen door so the cat could go in and out. He could smell the bread toasting and he took it out of the pan, smeared on some honey and ate it. It was the best honey, Florence's cousin had sent it from some part of France where it was special, and she never wanted to use it, save it. For what? he thought.

The phone rang. He looked at the clock instinctively. If anyone phoned before eight Florence would really get mad, tell them immediately where they'd gone wrong, even her best friends. It was only six twenty-five. Even as he was moving toward the phone he realized he didn't have to answer. That's what the machine was for. The phone shrilled five times, then intoned Florence's voice. "We're not able to answer the phone right now. Leave your name and number and a message." Years ago someone had told Florence not to say they weren't home, because it was only burglars, checking, so they could come and rob you. So she never said "We're not home." It shocked him to hear her voice, as if it was an offense to nature, once she was gone, to leave an echo. Right away he determined to change the message, and he picked up the folder with the directions for the answering machine. But he couldn't understand anything it said, she'd always done the message, and besides, he had nothing to say to people who phoned. So he just unplugged the answering machine and plugged the phone right into the wall. The way it used to be, most of his life, before answering machines.

As if challenging him, the phone rang again. His instinct told him to pick it up, but he was stubborn. He thought that if you gave him an hour he couldn't think of anyone he wanted to talk to just now. So he let it ring, ten, twenty times, then he got mad, just picked up the receiver and put it down again. The dim light on the shades in the living room bothered him. Florence had installed shades on the tall windows so the sun never came in. The sun would bleach the rugs, she said, and the books in the bookcase. He'd always liked to see the trees outside, so he pulled up the blinds and let the world come in. It was great.

When he sank back in his chair again the sun was glinting off the plaque on the wall. It was his familiar plaque, hanging up, the dark green plush with his memorabilia mounted on it. It always gave him a good feeling. In the left upper corner was an old photo of him waving a AK-47, one he'd taken out of the bunker that day, the day he'd won the medal. Next was his combat infantry badge, the long blue rectangle with the silver rifle in it. Then his Bronze Star—the medal for bravery. Underneath were a few other old photos, sort of yellowed now, him and his buddies over there. Mostly they were drinking, waving at the camera. Florence hated his plaque. The war's over, she'd say. We could put a nice picture there. But that was his life, he'd told her, his life before real estate. There were his sergeant stripes, cut out and pasted on the plaque. A sergeant. Who knows what a sergeant is these days? he thought. And then he realized he'd forgotten to make coffee.

Sitting there he remembered there were no beans left. He'd meant to go to Coffee Roasters yesterday, get a couple of pounds of

Starting All Over Again 125

espresso. But he'd forgotten. Florence always wanted him to get the mocha blend, it was lighter and the espresso was too strong for her. But she drank mostly tea and he loved the dark espresso. He thought about going to Coffee Roasters now. There was this cute girl there, Laurie, who always made such a big deal when he came in. "Henry! I missed you, honey! Two pounds of espresso again?" She was so...perky. Perky, that was the word. Once she had patted him on the face. Her little hands, her delicate little fingers had sent a shock through his cheek. He'd had fantasies ever since then about Laurie. What if he asked her to go to Las Vegas for the weekend? He'd give her lots of money to gamble, maybe go shopping, buy a wardrobe. What would she do when they were alone in the hotel room, maybe one of those rooms you could get with a jacuzzi, steam coming up, floating in there together naked? He was imagining it, just in the back of his mind. He thought, sure, go to Las Vegas with Laurie! How about going to Mars with Madonna? Just about as likely! But why should he be negative?

Henry stared at the wall facing him, looking for inspiration. He could see the desert stretching before them on the I-15, the road to Vegas. He'd gone there before, ages ago, with Florence. Okay, forget Florence, this is about Laurie. Let's see, she had a, not a great figure, but petite, you could see the little nenes in there against her T-shirt, even a little nipple, he remembered, the last time he'd been there in the coffee shop and wondered if she had a bra on. Laurie in Las Vegas! He stared at the wall, seeing the long, empty freeway, the desert, the light tan mountains in the distance with the light on them from the sun behind him. And the road kept going up and up....

There was a sound of a car coming in on the gravel outside in the driveway. A car door slammed. Then there were heavy footsteps in the gravel, then clacking on the concrete walk. A key turned in the door and Florence walked in.

"Henry? Why is the cat outside? Are you crazy? You know what happened to Climber!" There was the sound of parcels being put down on the kitchen counter. "And what's my begonia doing out in the garden? Henry? And you got the blinds up! Don't you know what that'll do to the rugs? I've been telling you and telling you...."

Florence stopped in front of Henry in his chair. He was a man at peace, his eyes open, staring at the wall in front of him, a little smile on his face.

"Oh, my God!" said Florence. She looked at Henry, then looked at the wall he was staring at. Her eyes focused on the plaque. She looked back at Henry, then at the plaque again. She frowned. Then she quickly took the plaque off the wall and jammed it down into the wastebasket behind Henry's chair.

The phone rang. Florence picked it up.

"Hello?...Yes. Hi, Betty!...You did?...And then he hung up?... Listen, Betty! You're not going to believe this!" Her face was alive with excitement.

The Long Way to Tuscany

It had rained during the night, but the day dawned impossibly beautiful, the bluest of blue Mediterranean skies, perfectly clear with the new sun just peeking over the Alps to the northeast. *Maybe it's just because we're never up at this hour,* thought Jane. They'd come into Milan on the plane last night from Frankfurt, and JFK before that. They'd fallen into bed at the hotel like dead people and woke promptly at five o'clock, victims of jet lag. So they decided to go for a walk at six, and it was marvellous, hardly any traffic in the streets, air still fresh, smelling like the orange blossoms on the trees along the boulevard, the streets clean from the rain.

By eight-thirty they'd breakfasted, packed up, and were on the autostrada heading south in their little rental car, the green Fiat, luggage in the trunk where it couldn't be seen by thieves, as the agent had advised them.

They were driving through green fields, immature in the springtime. The farmhouses were funny looking, not like little family farm homes back in America, but massive, looking almost like warehouses, but centuries old, peach-colored, with tiled roofs, tractors standing in the yards, fields and houses protected by rows of poplar trees.

Jane was eating it up with her eyes. The strangeness, the beauty. Neither of them had been in Europe before, and now Dick had five weeks of sick leave after being badly hurt on the job. Dick's friend Tony had said, "You guys gotta go to Italy, man! You'll love it!" And he'd recommended an agency that specialized in rentals in Tuscany. Villas, they called them, but they were really cottages, by the week, a good price before the summer season really started. The agency gave them a package: airfare, rental car, and a month in this villa. Dick was actually Italian, their name was Santi, but he'd never been here and his parents hadn't let the kids learn Italian. "We're Americans now," they'd told Dick, and he'd regretted it ever since, especially on his job, with so many Italians to deal with there in New York.

As Jane was looking at Dick sitting there in the driver's seat with a smile on his face two, three cars with German license plates went screaming by them in the fast lane.

"I don't believe those guys!" said Dick. "I thought we were going fast, but they must have been going a hundred or more! I wonder if it's just Germans, or if all the Europeans drive that way?"

"I read that it's all the same speed limit now, a hundred and thirty kilometers an hour everywhere, now that they're all like one country, don't even need passports or anything," said Jane.

Dick's face instantly froze in terror.

"My God! What's wrong, babe?"

"When you said passports! I just realized. I gave my passport to the hotel clerk last night, and I forgot to get it back this morning. Oh, shit!"

"Well, it's no big deal, Dicky. Next exit get off, go on back. We'll still get to Pienza by lunch, if we hurry."

The Long Way to Tuscany 129

But Dick had seen a police turnaround on the autostrada.

"I'll do it even quicker," he said.

"I don't know if we're supposed to use this...." Jane was saying, but Dick had already whipped the little car around the turn and was going back the other way on the toll road.

The ticket taker at the offramp on the outskirts of Milan was not helpful. He looked with disbelief at their toll ticket, which was supposed to be going in the other direction, and pointed them at a parking slot by the police office. There they had to wait over a quarter of an hour. Dick finally peeked around the door and saw three policemen in snappy uniforms watching what seemed to be a daytime soap opera on the television. He cleared his throat, got annoyed looks and a babble of argument among the three men. Finally the evident loser of the argument got to his feet and came outside. The ticket taker yelled something from his booth, and the policeman nodded. Dick tried to explain what had happened in his few words of Italian. The policeman obviously had no intention of understanding.

"Passport," he demanded.

"Ah! Passport! In hotel! Milano!" said Dick desperately, pointing toward the center of the city in the distance.

The policeman said nothing but strode over to the little coffee shop next to the toll booths. He was some time before returning with an old man wearing an apron. He indicated that Dick should tell his story again to the old man.

"Aha! Americans," said the old man. "How you doin'? I worked in Trenton, New Jersey. Twenty years. So you leave the passport in hotel! Old problem!" And he cackled. "You have to go back, no?"

"We have to go back, yes," said Jane, with growing irritation. "So, will they let us go now?"

The old man rapidly explained the situation to the policeman, who burst explosively into a long tirade directed at the old man, then looked grimly at the Santis.

"He say, you gotta pay lost ticket."

"But we didn't lose the ticket," said Jane. "It's right here in your hand!"

"No. Lost ticket from Firenze—Florence. You coming from direction Florence, you have to pay ticket from Florence!"

They both protested, but the policeman was adamant. Finally Dick pulled out his wallet with resignation and asked how much.

"Jesus!" he said to Jane, after figuring it out. "That's almost forty dollars! And I don't have enough liras."

Cambio qua, said the policeman, pointing at the coffee shop.

"Yes, we change money. Good rates," said the old man, leading them to the shop.

"This rate is terrible," said Jane, looking at the handwritten chart over the coffee shop cash register. "It's about two thirds what we should be getting for a hundred-dollar traveler's check! Thirteen hundred? It should be about two thousand at least!"

"Screw it," said Dick. "Let's pay up and get outta here." But back at their car there was no sign of a policeman. The attraction of the soap opera had won out.

Jane looked around rapidly. The ticket taker was bogged down with a long line of cars.

"Come on, babe. Let's just go. We're really not stealing or anything. We were on their dumb highway about five minutes, is all. We head back to the hotel, we can still be back on the road in a half-hour." And they took off back down the access road toward Milan.

But it was not to be so. The one-way streets that had been so helpful leading them directly to the autostrada now took them every direction except back to their hotel. Finally Dick managed a shortcut by backing up one one-way street and then brazenly driving the wrong way up another street for four blocks, ignoring oncoming cars blaring their horns and swerving up onto the sidewalk when necessary.

They parked in the loading zone at their hotel, and Jane ran in to get Dick's passport.

The Long Way to Tuscany   131

"Oh, *signora*, I'm so sorry!" said the clerk. "I was not on duty last night, I didn't know the passport was yours. The police come every morning and we cannot keep passports. They take them downtown if there is no person."

"Oh, my God!" said Jane. "We'll have to drive down to the police station?"

"No, no!" the clerk was firm. "Impossible to drive. The *centro*, the center of town is crazy. And nowhere at all to park. You must take taxi! Tell him, the *questura*."

Jane and Dick conferred. "I'll take a cab to the police station, the *questura*, whatever," he said. "You stay here and keep an eye on the car and the luggage."

A taxi obligingly turned into their street, Dick hailed it and, with a grin and a wave, was off to the crazy *centro*.

Jane sat in the car for a bit, looking at the road map and trying to figure how far they would get by lunchtime if Dick took half an hour, or an hour, or more. Then she realized there was a big Mercedes right behind her and that their little Fiat was right in the middle of the loading zone. So she moved to the driver's seat and pulled the car up almost to the street. It wasn't enough. In a minute the clerk came out.

"I'm so sorry, *signora!* We have many people coming. Could you maybe find some other place to park?"

Jane looked at the street. It was jammed with parked cars, even double-parked in places.

"I...I don't think there is any place. Look, I'll just move the car when people pull in. Okay?"

The clerk looked dubious but he went back into the hotel. Then, about five minutes later, a slender, elegant man in a beautiful light tan suit came out of the hotel and right over to the car.

"*Signora,*" he said. "Carlo told me of your difficulty. But I think we can help you. A special favor. We have a private parking behind the hotel. I have told Carlo it is perfectly all right for you to park there. It is very safe, with a locked gate, and then you can sit in the hotel."

"Oh, that's wonderful!" said Jane. "Just point me in the direction."

"Well, up there, at the end of the block, there is a *senso unico*, how you say?"

"One-way street," said Jane. It was one of the phrases they had been told to memorize.

"Yes. One-way. So you have to go left, instead of right at the corner, then the next block it is again a one-way...."

The gentleman was obviously thinking hard. Then he made up his mind.

"Is simple if I drive the car, okay? No problem then. I meet you at the back of the hotel. There is a door to the parking."

Jane was relieved. She hadn't driven in Italy yet and wasn't sure she wanted to, what she'd seen so far. She handed over the keys gratefully. There was just a moment of apprehension as she saw their little green Fiat, and all their luggage, going off down the street with a man whose name she didn't even know. Then she chided herself for her mistrust. He had an elegant suit, he'd just come out of the hotel, he must be a manager or something. So she walked back into the hotel, down the long hall leading to the back, and found a blind intersection, short halls leading to left and right, no obvious door to the parking outside. She ventured down one hall and found a dead end. Then, pulse rate mounting, to the end of the other branch, where she encountered two maids with their cart, one a dusky brunette, the other very black. They were busily cleaning a recently occupied room.

"*Prego,*" she said, using one of her fifteen Italian words. "Where is the door to the parking?"

The two ladies were friendly, trying to help, but it was obvious that there was little comprehension.

"Parking, parking!" she repeated, pointing towards the back wall, willing her finger to penetrate the wall and register some under-

The Long Way to Tuscany   133

standing. She'd seen signs in Milan already that said "parking" and knew that it was a universal word.

The ladies looked at the back wall, conferred rapidly with each other in a babble of Italian, then the older, matronly lady left the cart, took her by the arm and led her back up to the entrance, saying firmly, "Reception, reception, *signora*," smiling in a exaggerated way, as if reassuring an idiot.

There she met the clerk with a face so devoid of understanding that she somehow knew what had happened. But she asked the question anyway.

"Where is the door to the hotel parking, in back?"

She knew, she knew, before the words were said. *There is no hotel parking. Where did she leave her car?*

When she finally admitted that she had given the keys to their car to a stranger, the words coming out with hopeless resignation, the clerk could not at first believe his ears.

"You gave the keys to your car to a strange person?"

"Yes, but he came out of the hotel. And he had on a light tan suit. I thought he was the manager or something."

"*Signora!* You cannot give your keys to someone you do not know!"

His tone made her a little mad. "But he came out of the hotel. You must have seen him! A thin man, older, good-looking, with a nice tan suit?"

By this time there were several hotel employees gathered, listening in on what promised to be an entertaining conversation. The clerk turned to them and started a long, explosive dialogue. Jane could see the gestures, the height of the man, his slimness, the fine suit, all explained in staccato Italian and accompanying sign language. At least everyone nodded. They knew the man.

The clerk turned back to her, sighing. "Yes, *signora*, the man came out of the hotel. But he was only asking to reserve a room. We told him we were, how you say, *complet*, and he left."

Jane thought quickly. "But how did he know what I was doing out there on the driveway?"

Once more, conferring. "Yes. Yes, *signora*. He said he wished to bring his car up and we told him you would have to move out of the way."

Jane was a big girl, so she didn't collapse in tears. But she had to grope her way back to the little lounge in the reception area and sit down with her head in her hands. She was trying to figure out what to do, but the situation was so impossible that she was beyond thought. All she could do was inventory the contents of the suitcases. The clothes, the books, the few kitchen items and favorite knives she had brought along to cook marvelous Tuscan food—and then she remembered the attaché case that was in there, with the thousands of dollars in travelers checks and...all the rental papers for the villa...and her passport, now in the same limbo as Dick's. She wondered, idly, if it was worth trying to get the clerk to call the central police station, to try to intercept Dick, but it just seemed all so hopeless, so hopeless....

Dick looked up at the large, dirty, faceless building in the noisy madness of downtown Milan. He didn't know where to start, so he just walked in and looked for a directory, the kind they would have in New York in any public building. Nothing. There was a man at a small desk by the entrance who was looking at him curiously, so he walked over and asked if he spoke English. The man unleashed a long sentence of Italian that seemed to mean that he didn't, but that he would try to find someone who could. At least he was smiling and pleasant.

A small man in a suit eventually turned up. He didn't speak English either, but Dick managed to say "Passport, passport," with enough feeling to make the man nod, take his arm, and guide him to an elevator.

"Five. Five!" said the little man. But he wouldn't get on the elevator with Dick.

The Long Way to Tuscany   135

On what Dick would have thought of as the sixth floor the elevator stopped and he got out facing a long counter, familiar in every
bureaucracy in the civilized world, manned by too few personnel,
with too many people standing in line. Dick obediently took a place
in what he thought was the shortest line and waited, and waited, and
waited. After about a half-hour he'd had enough. Jane had often
cautioned him about his temper, but in his line of work he often
found that it helped. He walked over to the counter and made his
own line.

"Hey!" he shouted with some force. "I'm looking for my passport!"

The man at the counter at whom he was yelling looked at him
with contempt and gestured at the back of the line.

"No!" Dick shouted. "You people have my passport, and I want it
now!"

The commotion triggered the appearance of several uniformed
officers from a back room. They rapidly surrounded Dick and he realized he was being treated like any other disruptive person wandering into a structured environment. A mean-faced cop looked him in
the eye and demanded, "Passport! Give me passport!"

"I don't have my passport. *You* have my passport!" Dick was doing his best to point back into the office, where he hoped his passport lay somewhere.

The policemen conferred. Then one stepped forward.

"You have other identification?" he said in labored English.

Dick had been told that American driver's licences meant nothing in Europe. But he did have credit cards. So he pulled out his old
leather wallet, put it on the counter, opened it and heard a gasp of
amazement.

It took him a second to realize that they were all looking at his
buzzer—the badge in his wallet that was inscribed NYPD.

A moment of silence was broken by a question from the circle of
onlookers.

"You are *En Why Pee Dee?*"

Dick heard the disbelief in the questioner's voice and wondered if he was in bigger trouble. First no passport, then impersonating a police officer. And now from an inner office came a short, broad man in civilian clothes. He had a hard, flat face under sparse, curly, dark hair. The short sleeves of his shirt revealed massive, hairy forearms. And he was angry. He shouted what were obvious obscenities at the crowd that was being entertained, then turned on Dick.

"What is your business here? Are you making trouble?"

Dick started to explain about his passport, relieved to find an English speaker, but a babble of Italian from the other policemen interrupted him.

The newcomer now scrutinized the open wallet and the detective's badge. He looked up with suspicion.

"You are policeman?"

"Well, yeah. Detective."

"You have other identification? Everyone here watches this NYPD show on television. You think no one ever pretends to be NYPD cop?"

As usual Dick just got mad himself. Looking around he spotted one of the other skeptics laughing, a man in semi-uniform with a handcuff holder on his belt. Time for action.

"Yeah. I have ID. Let me show you." He turned to the man with the handcuffs and held out his hand. "Could I see those for a minute?" he asked with studied politeness. Surprised, the policeman handed him the cuffs. In a split second Dick slapped one cuff on one of the man's hands, spun him around, and cuffed both hands behind his back, yelling, "You have the right to remain silent..." the litany of the Miranda warning.

Once again there was a moment of silence. Then everyone started speaking at once, some of them yelling humorous abuse at the handcuffed cop, the victim shouting back at them to release him.

The Long Way to Tuscany   137

There was now a huge audience of civilians who had been standing
in line, forming an appreciative circle, glad to postpone their business for a show.

Hairy forearms just smirked. "That was a good move, or maybe
you practiced a lot. What brings you to Italy, Mr...." and he consulted the wallet, "Mr. Santi? Santi? You're Italian? And you don't
speak Italian? Or maybe you just have Mr. Santi's wallet? Eh?"

Jane had gone into the small ladies' toilet in the lobby of the hotel to
wash her face and try to pull herself together. It wasn't working very
well. She had a moment of panic and collapsed in tears on the tiny
settee. She lost track of time until a voice began to register in her
consciousness. "*Signora*...please, *signora?*"

She looked up. It was the black maid, reaching out hesitantly to
touch her shoulder.

"I'm...I'm sorry. I didn't hear you."

"*Signora*. I should tell you something...."

"But...you speak English?"

"Yes. I learn in school back in...back where I come from."

Jane couldn't imagine how a black woman in Italy would know
English. Or why there was a black woman in Italy, for that matter.
"Where...where did you come from?"

"Ethiopia. Was part of Italy, you know, long time ago, so my
mother came to Italy. More jobs. And we learn English back in
Ethiopia. Everyone wants to know English, go to America, England." Her face was alive. Jane felt a sudden relaxation of tension,
having someone to talk to in English.

"I'm so relieved there's somebody I can talk to! Tell me, what's
your name?"

"Is Miriam. You know, like in Bible?"

"Miriam. Yes. Okay. Also like in America, Miriam. A nice name.
My name is Jane. And what...?"

"Miss Jane? I heard Carlo say, about the passport, about the car?"

Jane suddenly realized that this woman knew something about her big problem.

"Yes? What do you know? Please tell me!"

"It's very simple," Dick was saying. He had taken a business card out of his wallet and was holding it out to his inquisitor. "You call my precinct at this number and ask who Dick Santi is. They'll tell you. And here…" he pulled a wad of lire out of his pocket, the same lire he had avoided paying out at the toll booth on the autostrada. "Here, this should cover your phone bill."

The Italian policemen looked at each other questioningly, and one pointed at his watch and started to say it was the middle of the night in New York.

"Excuse me?" Dick burst out. "You close up here at night? I'm sorry, pal. The bad guys don't close up in New York. I can tell you my watch commander who's on duty right now." He consulted his watch. "Five-thirty in the morning, it's Sergeant Blomberg. So go ahead, call, and ask him about Dick Santi!"

The head cop gave Dick a hard stare, then, carefully, instead of phoning the number on Dick's card he called New York information, got the same number, spoke with Sergeant Blomberg, and then entertained the whole office with a long story. He accompanied his tale with many gestures, including obvious discharges of firearms. Then he pushed the money back at Dick. "No charge for the phone, detective. So tell us all about the shooting. Your sergeant says you were a hero."

The Ethiopian woman was in turmoil, Jane could tell. Her face was contorted, turned to the restroom door, anticipating a sudden interruption to their conversation. Finally she summoned her courage.

"I think Carlo is bad man. I think he helps the other man steal cars."

Jane was shocked. "Steal? He helped steal my car?"

The Long Way to Tuscany 139

"Yes, *signora*. I know he did something like this two times this week. Both times foreign, like you. Some story about parking. And with that other man."

Jane was trying to comprehend. Could there actually be collusion between the clerk and the car thief? When she thought about it, it seemed logical. But the passport? What could they have done…"

"And the passport, *signora*, I have to tell you, the police do not come to take the passports."

Jane came quickly to life. Now she had an idea of what was going on, she could do something about it.

"Miriam, can we call the police station, whatever they call it, the *questura*, see if my husband is there? Will you help me?"

"I said I would help you, *signora*. I was afraid I will lose my job. That's why I didn't speak before. But now I know I must tell the truth." She came to Jane, took both her hands.

"*Signora*, I maybe lose my job, but don't let them hurt me, will you?"

Jane was getting steamed up. "Miriam, you just stick with me. Nobody's going to hurt you!" And she stormed out of the bathroom, headed for the reception desk.

Down at the *questura* Dick was surrounded by a crowd of admirers. He had his shirt pulled up and he was explaining the angry, red eight-inch scar on his left side.

"See, my partner Tony kicked in the door…*boom*! He's a big dude, know what I mean? Then I'm first in the room, and I'm yelling 'Police! Police! Freeze!' and everyone freezes, except this one guy, cool as a cucumber, lifts up his niner and it's like I can even see the fucking bullet coming. *Wham!* It hits me in the side and I'm like, 'This is it, I'm fucking dead, after all these years!' And I'm on the floor. And then I hear *boom*, and it's Tony blowing away the sucker with his shotgun. So they get me to the hospital and they're trying to fix the hole it went in when the doctor goes, 'Wait a minute,' and they turn me over and he finds the hole it went out, and there was like major damage. But I gotta hand it to those guys. They put me back together like I was the six-million-dollar man, you know what I'm saying?"

The guy with hairy forearms, whose name turned out to be Mario, was translating for the rapt audience when a woman came out of the inner office and called him away. Now Mario returned with a puzzled look on his face.

"Detective...."

"Uh, call me Dick, please."

"Okay. Detective Dick, the *carabinieri* just called from the *autostrada*. They say they have a rental car in the name of Richard Santi, they stopped it and arrested the man driving it. They were looking for the car because... Did you drive off without paying earlier today?"

"Well, yeah. Maybe. Listen, it's a long story. But what the hell is my car doing out there? Listen, I gotta find out what happened to my wife!" Dick was getting panicky. "Can we call the hotel from here?"

"Come, we call from the car. They recognize the man, a thief. And much valises with your name in back. We go!"

Jane and Miriam were coming out of the bathroom, preparing to confront Carlo at the desk when they saw him on the telephone. Whatever he was hearing made him go pale, and without a word he hung up and walked out the hotel door.

"What was that all about?" Jane started to ask, but just then the phone rang again. Miriam sprinted across the lobby and answered in Italian. Jane could hear her saying *Si, si, signore*...and then she handed the phone to Jane. It was Dick.

"Babe! Thank God!" he was saying. "I just found out about our car. And I thought something had happened to you. So how the hell—?"

The Long Way to Tuscany   141

But Jane interrupted. "*You* found out about the car? What about the car?" And finally they both slowed down and explained their adventures, Jane rather sheepishly about giving her car keys to a stranger.

"No, no, babe, don't feel bad," Dick was saying. "It's an old con, and a good one and lotsa smarter people than you been taken that way, right on the streets of New York."

"But what if...what if I'd stayed in the car with him?"

"He'd have found a way to get you out. Fender bender, ask you to get out, check the damage, anything, he drives off! I've seen this before. The guy's not inventing the wheel, you know! Now what you gotta do is come out to the *autostrada*. I'm on the police car phone right now. Mario here is taking me with him, but he says there's no time to pick you up. Wrong direction. So can you grab a cab and meet us out there? We can finally leave, get to Pienza this afternoon. Mario says it's hard to get a cab this time of morning, but I'll just wait here if you have trouble."

"But what about your passport?"

"Mario says the cops never pick up the passports anymore, if they ever did. Are you standing at the desk? Look through any drawers they got there. I saw the guy put it in last night."

Jane rummaged quickly through the drawers in front of her. She found one full of passports, but no Richard Santi.

"Yours isn't here. Carlo must have taken off with it."

"Well, no big deal. Now the locals know our story we can get another from the consul before we leave. How about your passport?"

"I just hope it's still in the car, with our luggage."

"Our luggage. Jesus, let's hope so. Anyway, gotta go. See you out on the *autostrada*."

As Jane hung up she realized she'd been hearing a horn honking persistently for the last few minutes. Now the noise-maker himself entered the lobby, a large man with a red face, wearing a black suit. He zeroed in on her, there behind the counter.

"Vere is ze bellboy? I am vaiting a half-hour already!"

Jane had a sudden inspiration. "Oh *signore*, I am so sorry," she said, hoping her Italian accent wasn't too over the top.

"Miriam!" she called. "Please to carry the *signore's* bags. And I make Carlo to park the gentleman's car in our parking."

Why the hell should I try to find a taxi, she was thinking. *We've wasted enough time already.*

New York Jews

New York Jews who are writers are always writing about what it's like to be a Jewish writer in New York. Well, as all the books say, write what you know about. Anyway, since half the magazines in the country are published in New York I have this picture in my mind of editors looking at stories set in Santa Monica or Dallas or anywhere—Spearfish, South Dakota, you name it—and they read one paragraph and say, "Nah! Where's the Angst?" It's a tough market to crack. I got the rejection slips to prove it. So when I was explaining this to a woman friend she said, "Well then, Petey, instead of just complaining why don't you write about what it's like being a gentile writer here in the Valley? Maybe there's a market for that." So I go, "Sure! How many people you know here in the Valley read anything?" and she goes, "Women do, dummy! Don't you know that women buy eighty percent of the books in this country?" And I'm like, "Come on!" so she goes, "*Cosmo*'s got a circulation of around three million. *Esquire*? 750,000, I looked it up. That's only one quarter of—"

"Hah!" I break in, "How about *Playboy*?" and she goes "Men don't buy *Playboy* to read, they buy it to beat off." Well, I wasn't going to argue with that, so we discussed it some more and finally I agreed I'd write something about what it was like being a writer in the Valley.

I always wanted to write. Actually, what I originally wanted when I first started was not so much to do the writing part of it but to be a Writer and be famous and meet babes at parties because my friend Mort told me his older brother was a screenwriter and once they were shooting his script and this sort of minor actress wanted a bigger part and more dialogue and he acted dumb and said, "Uh, what lines would you want where?" and she said "Come on to my trailer, and I'll give you some ideas." And Mort's brother gives us a knowing look and rolls his eyes around, meaning we're supposed to believe he got awesomely laid, which I don't believe because between his bald spot and his big gut he could've given her twenty pages of Tennessee Williams and still not gotten laid. But anyway. Anyone can write, but being a Writer means that at a party if you're introduced to a woman as a Writer and she asks, "Oh yeah? What have you written?" you can say, "Well, Harper Collins published my *Last Offramp to Redondo,* and Bantam is dickering for the paperback rights, but if they can't do better than a mil-five I'll go to auction." Actually, I couldn't say that because I'm publishing almost exclusively these days in only two magazines, and if I told any reasonably intelligent female at a party what the magazines are she'd find she had to go out to the kitchen to get some more onion dip. But I do make a pretty good living. Fifteen years ago, when I dropped out of Cal State Northridge to try writing full time, I sent stories everywhere, from *The New Yorker* and *Atlantic Monthly* to *Christian Maturity*. I'd hang out in the magazine section at this big bookstore and read all the mags and get an idea what kind of material they wanted and then try to adapt my style. I really did sell a story to *Christian Maturity* (that used to be *Young Christian,* but their subscribers were really loyal) and believe it or not, one to *Romance and Gourmet* under the name Felicia Pandolfi. That was after *Dating Scene* was bought by *Dining World*. But I never cracked the big-ticket mags, and I was getting more and more published at these two other magazines, so I just decided that's where my future was.

So now I guess I have to confess that the two magazines I mainly write for are *BIKER!* and *Big Breasted Babes*. Okay, I know you're not going to believe that bikers actually read magazines or that there's a mag called *Big Breasted Babes,* either one. But just look up the headings in *Periodical Markets for the Modern Writer* and there they are. You see, I was going through that book alphabetically, mainly to see what they were paying per word or per page, and under the Bs I found those two and they paid pretty well and I sold the first submissions I sent in. So I finally decided to specialize, and by now *they* phone *me* up and say, "Got anything new, Petey?" Best thing is, they're both bi-weeklies, so they always need material. For *BIKER!* you have to tell stories about guys with Harleys who are either heroes in some violent situation or who score with awesome babes in some totally unrealistic scenario. *Periodical Markets* tells the aspiring writer that *BIKER!* wants violent heroics or erotica, no fantasy or sci-fi, but I'm telling you that what these guys want is really fantasy, something that'll convince a biker with a huge hairy gut and six months' worth of B.O. that if he beats up a guy wearing a suit who is supposedly "bothering" a waitress with ten-ton tits that he can score some steamy sex because of her gratitude. Is that science fiction or what? Real fantasy, you get a look at some of those guys. *Big Breasted Babes* has a lot of photographs of you-know-what and they want just a few stories every week to suggest some imaginative situations you could get into with a big-breasted babe, because most of the guys who read this mag don't have much imagination and so they look at the photos until their mouths are flapping open and then here's this story right next to the photo that starts, "Gavin let his tongue roll around Chantal's erect nipples until her moaning got too intense…" and then these guys think, "Hey, I could do that!" and they actually read the story, which has got to be pretty short and to the point. I can write about three of those in an afternoon and at four hundred bucks a story it's easy work.

A funny thing. One day a woman phoned me up and asked for Monique. At first I thought it was a wrong number, but then I remembered I had written a story under the name Monique Glide. It started out with a guy in a typical Valley singles bar asking a babe what her sign was, and she said, Slippery When Wet, and it went on from there. Anyway, I wasn't going to admit that I was Monique Glide, but this woman was very insistent and I wanted to find out what kind of woman wanted to talk to the author of a dumb story about a big-breasted babe who said her sign was Slippery When Wet, so I finally confessed that I was Monique Glide. And she hollered, "I knew it, only a man could write bullshit like that! Aren't you ashamed of yourself?" And I said, like I say to relatives, it's a living and it's only fantasy and I'm sorry you were offended, because believe it, she was offended, you know what I mean? I thought she'd hang up, but she kept going on, what kind of a chauvinist pig can write garbage like this for a living and I told her that I'm actually considered a nice guy and that I could give her referrals from several women who know me. And she goes, "Sure! And do they all have big tits?" So I got a little hot myself and I go, "What I do for a living has nothing to do with who I am," and then I asked, "What do you do for a living?" and it turned out she was a paralegal working for a big personal injury law firm there in the Valley, and I said, "Well, there you go!" and I could tell she was trying to decide whether to hang up or laugh but we talked about it a bit and she finally laughed and that's how I met Barbara and we had some great times.

But about then the big crisis in my life came along. In my professional life, that is, because I got two letters the same day. One was from the publisher of *BIKER!* and the other was from my editor at *Big Breasted Babes,* and the letters were identical because actually they were just a printed handout, and they said, "To all vendors, advertisers, creditors, and contributors. Be advised that of August 31st the two magazines *BIKER!* and *Big Breasted Babes* have been purchased by Finian Mudrick Publications. Because of excessive overhead the publishers have decided to combine the two magazines, provisionally under the title of *Big Breasted Biker Babes!*" And in my envelope there was a note from my editor at *Babes* saying, "Petey, this title sucks! Can you come up with some other idea? We're not publishing until October." So you can imagine the pressure on me. Because this guy Finian Mudrick is a billionaire from Scotland who already owns about twenty American newspapers and magazines and a dozen TV stations and a movie studio, and I can just imagine while I am trying to write a story about big-breasted biker babes he's going to acquire *Arthritis Update* and *Koi Owner* and put them into the same magazine too. Bottom line, what I'm looking at is my income cut in half because there's no way I could write *all* the dumb stories in the new combined magazine.

The whole scene was getting complicated in other ways. Just a week before I got this news, the editors of *BIKER!* hired me to come out to sign T-shirts in Laughlin, Nevada, where the Harley guys have a convention every year. It was amazing, seeing two thousand Harleys parked in one place and these guys wandering the streets in all their getups and with their babes, and the hotel clerk said they were the least trouble of any convention they ever had. It surprised me, but it turned out some of the *BIKER!* readers had actually written in and said they liked the stories by Matt Barstow, or Doc Ramblin, or Mame Frazee, or some of the other names I used, and I could sit at a table and actually admit I was all those people and autograph black T-shirts with a silver ink felt pen for five bucks apiece. And that's where I realized the market was changing. Because I was hanging out in the bar with a couple of old-time bikers, guys with long gray ponytails and beards, listening to their old stories to get ideas, you know, keeping the Cuervo Gold flowing, and some dudes came up to the booth with humungous arms hanging out of their cutoff jackets, tatoos and all that, and it turned out they were like engineers and computer programmers and they were saying, hey man, we like the stuff you write but why don't you do some stories where bikers accidentally hack into some secret government computer, find out that there's a conspiracy to take over the country, so they get all their biker buddies together and attack the headquarters before it can get going, using laptops and cyber-sabotage and downloading viruses into the bad guys' mainframe, stuff like that? We're all sitting around in the bar of the Paddlewheel Radisson and these guys are getting more and more enthusiastic, and I go, "But that's just the plot of your *Saturday Night Movie* on Channel Thirteen!" and this bald guy, wearing all black leather, goes, "Hey! I'm the *producer* of *Saturday Night Movie* on Thirteen, fuhchrissakes! I'm dying for a good biker hero, all we get now are sci-fi or crud that went directly to video!" Well, you know he got my attention in a hurry. So I asked this guy, if I get a story published can you find a producer to make a TV movie of it? And he says, if I like the story, and I like all your stories. That's how I met Mike Radulescu, who really looked more like a biker than a Channel Thirteen movie producer, although the tatoos washed off, which is really sort of Channel Thirteenish.

Anyway, I wrote the story, and the bikers had cell phones and laptops built into their Harleys so they could communicate and solve complex situations and their informants were some waitresses at a Hooters bar in D.C. who had overheard some slimy guys conspiring to take over the government. And the final scene was when the bikers attacked a secret installation in Virginia and they had disabled the bad guys' electronics with their computers and, as you might guess, the waitresses from Hooters had already infiltrated, pretending to be models who were going to show a good time to the bad guys and their clients, who were rotten foreigners. And the hero at the last second cracked the code of the bad guy's mainframe,

New York Jews 149

which was about to set off a nuclear bomb under the Pentagon. And you can bet your ass that *Big Breasted Biker Babes!* published that story in their first issue.

So that's how I happened to be sitting in the office of Finian Mudrick one day, having been called to consult on making a movie of this piece of crap for his movie studio. He's a wiry little guy, doesn't talk very much. And he surprised me, he really did, because I figured him for a fast-buck guy, but he's saying, "Why don't we budget this film at around 90 mil, top stars, and lots of great special effects? You'll get billing as top writer."

But my reaction was, the subject matter will sell it to those dummies out there. So how about only *fifteen* mil, get network TV stars who've never been on the big screen to do it for next to nothing, everybody knows their names, spend the extra money on promotion, all the mouth-breathers who watch TV will come to the movie and then you can bring out a line of laptop computers based on the movie and even some designer biker clothes.

This guy Mudrick is staring at me through his yellow glasses he wears all the time and he doesn't say a thing for almost five minutes, and I'm thinking I'm going to have to go back to short stories for a living and in my mind I'm going over the plot for the next thing I might write for *Gay Christian Maturity*, which was a spinoff after the original mag failed. But then Mudrick goes, "If we go low-budget, could we set the final scene in Malibu? It's a lot cheaper than Virginia." And I go, "Sure," and he goes, "Can the bomb be under Hollywood? It'd be a lot more relevant." And I nodded, yeah, you got that one right, and then he asked the big question: "Could the bikers invading the secret installation have to work their way around pools full of deadly koi?"

And you know what? The son of a bitch had actually gone and bought *Koi Owner*, and I should just be grateful he didn't buy *Arthritis*-whatever too, because I sure wouldn't have known how to work that in. What really bothered me was that now I had to write new material for koi instead of starlets who might've done major favors for extra lines.

So that's why I'm writing this here in my hilltop villa in Bel Air that I bought with what I scored on the movie, which I lucked into because Finian Mudrick didn't think one percent of the gross was going to be very much. And there's a dividend I have to tell you about. If you're trying to sneak into this place don't get near the koi ponds. Because Mudrick had them bred special, just for the movie, which as you know grossed over a hundred mil here, where we like our bikers and big-breasted babes, but *three hundred* million in Japan, where they know their koi.

That last scene in the movie still haunts me.

The Frampton County
Drunk Driver Project

Peter Berry was relieved to see a cluster of lights ahead on the highway. He'd been driving through the most deserted part of this farm state for over five hours and was ready for a drink and something to eat before driving on another two hours to Wheatville, where he had meetings tomorrow. He passed a sign saying, FRAMPTON, COUNTY SEAT OF FRAMPTON COUNTY. Then he could see the usual grain silos looming by the side of the road, a grade crossing, a gas station that looked closed for the night, bugs swarming in the light over the pumps. It was late September, but still real hot and sticky.

Blue and orange neon beckoned ahead: DAGMAR 'N' ED'S BAR RESTAURANT.

Peter sighed with relief. He'd been tasting that first martini of the day for the last few hours. A cold, crisp martini, a big rare steak, and a house salad. That would get him to Wheatville in good shape, he thought.

Dagmar 'n' Ed's was half empty, a big barn of a room with a salad bar up against one wall, a little bar with no bartender that he could see, tables made of thickly resined hatch covers, impervious both to

151

stains and thirty years of improved interior design standards. A neatly uniformed waitress brought him a menu and a glass of water and asked him if he wanted coffee. Peter was used to this part of the country, so he didn't react with the shock he had felt the first time he had been offered coffee before dinner.

"No, thanks," he said, "but I see you have a bar, and I'd love a double Beefeater martini on the rocks." He almost slavered, just saying the words.

The waitress looked dubious. "Well, yes, sir. But I'll have to get you the hostess for your bar order."

Peter was expecting a cocktail waitress. Instead a tall, slim woman in a maroon gown glided up to his table. She had a long, handsome face, framed in unfashionably long, dark red, wavy hair, and large, dark eyes with long, long lashes. Peter guessed her age at late thirties, maybe even forty, but she was just stunning, looking strangely out of place in this little roadhouse in the middle of nowhere. She was smiling, in a professional hostess-like manner, but she seemed to be appraising Peter in a peculiarly intense way, almost as if she were a doctor meeting a new patient.

"Are you the Beefeater martini?" Her voice was low and musical, but there was something sharp and questioning in her tone.

"Yes, ma'am! I've been waiting the last hundred miles!" Peter gave her his best salesman's smile, hoping to start a little conversation, find out what this woman was all about.

Instead, she turned abruptly and left the room. The bar remained empty. In a minute the first waitress appeared with the smallest cocktail glass Peter had ever seen. Four, maybe five ounces, he guessed. With the ice and all he doubted there was even a whole ounce of gin in there. He tasted it. It was a superb martini, just what he'd been waiting for. But his second taste drained the glass. Peter decided to count to ten, calm down, and then called the waitress over. He looked rapidly through the menu and ordered.

"I'll have your ribeye steak with fries. Make that nice and rare.

The Frampton County Drunk Driver Project 153

And the dinner salad. Oh…and I'll have another martini while I'm waiting. You know, the first one I ordered was supposed to be a double." He held up the glass. "But you can see this is a tiny glass. No way it could be a double."

The waitress looked at Peter, then looked back at the empty door to the kitchen as if seeking guidance. "I'll send your order in, sir," she finally said.

It was at least five minutes before the tall hostess appeared again, once again carrying a tiny cocktail glass.

"Are you staying in our little town tonight, sir?" she asked. She was still holding the drink out of reach. Peter was thinking of lying about staying, but then he remembered he hadn't seen a motel. So he was honest.

"No, no. Sorry. Maybe some other time. But I've gotta push on to Wheatville tonight. Got sales meetings early in the morning, and I gotta be fresh." He gave her the full Peter Berry boyish smile that had sold five million dollars' worth of farm machinery over the last two years.

The hostess put the glass down but kept her hand on it. Peter noticed that she had extraordinary long, sinuous fingers, and striking red fingernails.

"You realize," she said, "that this is your second drink, and that it might very well bring your blood alcohol level over the legal limit of point-zero-six, in this state. You might not want to drive after dinner." She arched an eyebrow at him.

Peter Berry had been a traveling salesman for over twelve years. He loved the life, the old friends on the road, the new ones, the new towns, restaurants, hotels. And he loved a drink or two at the end of the day. Or at lunch, even, to mellow out the drive to the next town. He'd never had a ticket or an accident in his life. So he was getting a little hot at this nosy hostess.

"You know, years ago my mother told me not to have more than one drink a day. But you know, my mom is with the angels now, and you're not my mother." He smiled, to take the bite out of his words. "So could you just let a tired old salesman relax and enjoy his meal?"

Once again the hostess turned and left abruptly, but at the kitchen door she turned and scrutinized Peter briefly before leaving. Her look sent a chill up his spine.

Peter drank his second miniscule drink in one gulp. Then, to show he wasn't intimidated, he ordered a glass of the anonymous house red wine with his steak. He expected the hostess back, but the waitress silently brought him his wine. He had expected it to be some miserable screwtop jug wine but when he tasted it, it was amazingly good—dark red, good nose, complex, with a long finish. Peter ate his steak and salad, drank his wine, had a cup of coffee— also wonderfully strong—then paid his bill with a credit card and left a cash tip, as he always did, to save the waitress trouble. As she was counting the generous tip she looked at him sideways and murmured, "Careful driving out of here, sir. Cops can be fierce."

So as Peter walked out onto the dark parking lot he looked around carefully. For all he could tell the entire town was asleep at 8:40 in the evening. The cicadas were putting up a storm of sound in the hot night, but nothing else was moving. In the parking lot there were only three old cars, a dusty pickup, and a Volvo station wagon, all of them deserted, so far as he could see. Peter got behind the wheel of his car, started the engine, the air conditioner, then began to pull out of the parking lot. A flashing red light lit up the lot behind him, on top of the Volvo, and its headlights came on, blinding in his rear-view mirror. A siren sang once into the night, then burbled into silence as if daring him to run for it. Peter sighed and turned his motor off. He hadn't even gotten out of the parking lot.

"Could you get out of the car, sir?" There was a big, friendly, midwestern face at his window. Peter could see another man in uniform standing behind him. He got out quickly, wearing his salesman's smile.

"A Volvo station wagon police car? That's a new one on me," he chuckled. "Is there some problem, officer?"

The cop ignored the Volvo gambit. "Have you been drinking this evening, sir?"

"The size of the drinks in there I wouldn't exactly call it drinking." Peter was beginning to think this whole town was obsessed with drinking.

"Sir, we're going to have to check your blood alcohol level. It's just routine. Would you please get back in your car and drive it across the road, just over there? It's the sheriff substation."

This is really weird, thought Peter, but he obediently got into his car and drove across the road and parked outside a little one-story building, dark and anonymous, nothing betraying a connection to law enforcement. He was beginning to worry, but when the two men unlocked the door, turned on the lights, and led him in, he could see all the proper furniture, the bureaucratic counter, the fax machine, and two computers. There were even wanted posters on the wall.

The friendly-looking cop went over to a sinister black machine. It had a long hose and a mouthpiece on one end. The smaller cop stayed by the door, as if he expected Peter to make a run for it.

"Just breathe out into this mouthpiece for a five-count, if you will." The cop turned a switch and bright lights flashed from the machine, green, orange, and red. A dial lit up.

Peter had been breathalyzed before. But he'd never gone over the blood alcohol limit, mostly, he thought, because he was fairly large and his body soaked up the booze pretty well. He knew he couldn't have exceeded the limit back there in Dagmar 'n' Ed's so he stepped forward without fear and exhaled into the mouthpiece, which he was glad to see was new and disposable.

The machine clattered a moment, contemplated, then the red light came on and the dial swung to 0.077. He couldn't believe his eyes. "But…but…" he started to say.

The big cop had his arm now. "You're almost two hundredths over the limit, sir. We couldn'ta booked you back there in the parking lot, but you drove your car over here across the road, a state highway, didn't you? We got ourselves two choices here. We can book you as a DUI, or you can agree to a summary judgment. Then you can wait an hour, have a cup of coffee, and get out of here."

Peter figured he knew what a "summary judgment" was. It was just a shakedown. They'd take a hundred bucks, more or less, and let him go. He'd run into that in the deep South but he thought it was a little tacky for this squeaky-clean state. Still, they'd tricked him into driving onto a state highway, so he figured they were as dirty as any red-clay Alabama sheriff. He sighed.

"I'll take the summary judgment, officer."

"We thought you would. Now if you'll just step into the next room, we'll take your photo and get your signature on the papers."

"Isn't all this a little unusual, officer?"

"Nossir. We had a couple of serious accidents, some kids got hurt, and the whole county decided to crack down on drunk driving. Frampton County Drunk Driver Project. Zero tolerance. Now, I know you weren't much over the limit and they'd probably let you skate over there in Cedar County, Wheatville, whatever. But we got your zero tolerance here. Right over there in the next room, sir? If you could move along?"

The next room was windowless and virtually empty. There was a hip-high oak rail, cushioned on top, looking oddly like an altar, and a camera mounted on the wall opposite.

The big cop handed him a clipboard and a pen. "This here is your release, saying you accept summary judgment."

Peter signed it, wondering when the pitch for the quick cash would come.

"Now if you'll just step up to the rail, so you'll be in focus for the camera."

Peter stood close to the rail and was looking at the camera when

The Frampton County Drunk Driver Project   157

he realized that the smaller man had come up behind him, bent over, and quickly snapped his ankles to the rail with a pair of leather-covered clamps he hadn't noticed. Peter started to struggle.

"What the hell is going on here? Are you guys crazy?" But the big cop just put up one hand for silence.

"You just shut up, mister. You signed the release. Dagmar'll be here in a minute, time she gets off work."

"Dagmar? What the hell…you mean from the restaurant?"

"Yep. Dagmar Lindstrom. She's the undersheriff for this part of the county. And you don't want to get on her bad side, you know what I mean?"

Peter was going to ask if Dagmar was a tall woman in a gown, but just then the woman in question came through the door. She was still wearing her hostess gown, but her welcoming smile was gone. She now had a look of grim satisfaction. She gave Peter a cold look, then queried the two men in the room.

"You got my phone call?"

"Yes ma'am. Suspect had two drinks and wine. We were waiting for him in the lot."

"Did he sign the summary judgment?"

"Yes'm, he did. And he's locked in for the photo."

"All right. Let's take it."

A blast of light went off in Peter's eyes. Then the big cop hit a switch on the wall and the room lights turned from bright white to dark red. The tall woman walked directly in front of Peter and gazed into his eyes.

"Are you ready to accept your summary judgment?"

Peter was trembling, but he was able to stutter his offer. "I'll be glad to pay. Hundred bucks, whatever."

Undersheriff Dagmar Lindstrom slapped him in the face. His head flew back, and he could tell that she was ungodly strong.

"We don't accept bribes here in Frampton County." Her face was now longer than ever, set firmly in anger.

"I didn't mean to bribe...I only thought..." Peter was babbling in fear, he realized.

"Clifford! Jimmy!" demanded Dagmar. "Prepare the subject in judgment position!" Before Peter could react the big cop came in front of him, seized both of his wrists in a crushing grip and started to bend him over the rail. At the same time the smaller cop reached in front of Peter, quickly undid his belt, and pulled his pants and underpants down to his knees, leaving his bare behind exposed. There were two more leather restraints at the front of the rail, and Peter found himself bent double, his ankles bound on one side, his wrists fastened securely on the other. He started to cry.

"Ah! Mr. Berry," said the tall woman named Dagmar. "Don't fall apart on us. You are only accused of driving under the influence. The judgment is very mild." And then she uttered the words that chilled Peter's blood.

"Deputy Blanchard, Deputy White? Could you leave us alone for a minute?"

They left, and Peter was horrified to hear one of them giggling. Then came the moment of truth. Dagmar Lindstrom strode to a drawer in the only desk in the room and took out a paddle. Peter had belonged to a fraternity in college and had been paddled by serious, white, upper-middle-class sadists. But he instantly recognized the paddle as insignificant—not much larger than a ping pong paddle. For a moment he was relieved, although he could still feel his testicles out there totally exposed. If she hit him on the balls he would die, he told himself, and started crying again.

Her voice was marvelously soothing. "Now, now, Mr. Berry. You will only receive the standard ten spankings specified by the Frampton County Drunk Driver Act. Please get a grip on yourself!" And she began to spank him.

Whap! landed the first blow. Peter could scarcely believe he had been hit, the blow was so tame, compared to what he had expected.

Whap! whap, whap, whap! continued the spanking. Peter had to

The Frampton County Drunk Driver Project 159

admit that it was beginning to sting, but he harbored the secret thought that if these psychopaths were actually willing to get off on spanking him ten times with an inadequate paddle, he was going to escape virtually scot-free.

Whap! went the final blow and Peter let out a low moan of relief, trying to give the impression that he had really been hurt.

There was a moment of silence, then Dagmar came around in front where he could see her clearly in the red light. To his consternation he saw that she had slipped out of her gown and was in her underwear, a dark red bra and bikini. Dagmar was sweating, breathing hard, and smiling obscenely.

"Well, Mr. Berry! Do you think you'll be having more than one drink in this county again?" She slapped the paddle against her other hand with calculated brutality.

"Sheriff," gasped Peter Berry, twisting his head up to look at her. "If you'll let me get out of here, I promise you'll never see me in Frampton County again!"

Undersheriff Dagmar gave him a nasty grin. "Not so fast, Mr. Berry. You'll need at least another half-hour before we can let you loose on our roads again, what with your shameful addiction to alcoholic drinks. In the meantime, did you know that ingesting alcoholic beverages can cause swelling of the prostate?"

Peter started to moan and cry again, helplessly.

"Yes, yes! You definitely need a prostate examination! And did you know that I am also the County deputy health director? I'm licensed to do this kind of examination. And it's for your own good!" Dagmar appeared before Peter again and let him watch her squeeze a bead of jelly out of a tube onto her long middle finger, with its sharp red fingernail. Then she disappeared behind him. Peter whimpered helplessly. Then the finger entered his anus and he could feel it penetrating endlessly, climbing up into his vitals. The finger touched his prostate and there was a stab of pain. He screamed.

"Oh, Mr Berry! What a sissy you are! And you know that I have to feel every side of your prostate. Prostate cancer is not a joke, Mr. Berry!"

Peter thought that at one point he must have passed out as her long, red-tipped finger wandered around his nether regions. He was drenched in sweat as he finally heard her say, as from a great distance, "You may go now, Mr. Berry. You'll be glad to know your prostate is normal. And don't drink and drive in Frampton County again!"

A few minutes later the two cops reentered the room and released his leather restraints. Peter stood up gasping, his face tear-streaked. He wanted to say that he would sue in the highest court in the land, but he was terrified that he would be strapped down again, so he said nothing, but followed the cops to the outer office, where they gave him the keys to his car. As fast as he could he hobbled out to his car, cranked the starter, pulled out of the lot in front of the sheriff's station, and was gone.

The two cops were out on the porch watching his lights go off into the distance.

"That's the third this week," said the big cop. "You think he'll complain to somone?"

"I don't think so," said the smaller cop. "Who's he gonna call, the D.A.?"

"D.A.'s the guy who wrote the drunk driver law," said the big cop, chuckling. "No way he's going to make any waves."

"Well, it's Commissioner Bumberger then," said the little cop. "He's the only other guy in the county you could write to."

"Yeah, Commissioner Bumberger," laughed the big cop. "*That* man's got a problem! He's come out of Dagmar 'n' Ed's and been busted for drunk driving fourteen times already since last month. Man sure loves his summary judgment! Try again, Mr. Salesman!" They both roared with laughter and went back into the station.